KV-055-002

00 401 037 177

PROMISE OF REVENGE

PROMISE OF REVENGE

Lauran Paine

CHIVERS

British Library Cataloguing in Publication Data available

This Large Print edition published by AudioGO Ltd, Bath, 2012.
Published by arrangement with Golden West Literary Agency

U.K. Hardcover ISBN 978 1 4713 1115 4
U.K. Softcover ISBN 978 1 4713 1117 8

Copyright © 2010 by Mona Paine

All rights reserved

Printed and bound in Great Britain by
MPG Books Group Limited

Promise of Revenge

I

In the moonlight the roadway looked oddly strange. There was no life in it anywhere. Dark shadows lay heavily across store fronts, across roof lines, and along the plank walks beneath wooden overhangs. It dropped from eaves in its many overtones; in some places it was darker and deeper than in other places. In front of the Cowmen's & Drovers' Bank, for instance, the darkness had a cold, bright lining to it, because the moonlight was reflected from a large glass window with golden letters upon it. Everything that lived was shrouded in this black and silver, cold, strange world of absolute silence. West of town where low hills lay there was flat open country for perhaps six miles, then the rise and lift of running land frozen in motion; a man on horseback atop the nearest hill could see the valley as it was.

Beatty was the hub. Emanating outward

from Beatty were a dozen pale roads, the spokes. Around the valley, far out, were the hills, silver-tinted now in the pale light. It was a scene to put a man in mind of an immense wagon wheel. The man atop the hill shifted in his saddle. Then he moved again because a pinched nerve in his right hip reminded him of the old wound. He looped the reins, made a cigarette, lit it, and exhaled. The silence was as deep as it would be at the bottom of the sea. He smoked and looked down into the valley and remembered.

There was a fine iron bird bath in Judge Montgomery's front yard behind the gleaming picket fence. There was a swing there, too, where the judge's daughter had been playing the first time he'd seen her. There was the fine gold lettering on the bank window; the substantial brick courthouse that rose majestically where the old plaza had been, and always — except in bad weather — the flag atop its white-painted pole. And the people. The good and orderly people. Of course many of the faces would now be strange; some would have moved on; a few perhaps would have died; but in the main they would be the same people. Judge Montgomery, Banker Elihu Gorman, Moses Beach of the Beatty Mercantile

Company, Sheriff Tim Pollard — all the excellent, substantial citizens of Beatty.

The solitary rider's lips drew down at their outward corners. All the fine people of Beatty. He pushed out his cigarette against the saddle horn, took up the reins, and kneed his mount down off the hill, moving slowly and very deliberately as though forcing himself to relive each twisting, hurting part of some deep-seated memory.

The north-south stage road ran on ahead, so bright in the moonlight it seemed to glow. He rode out in plain sight, the only moving, living thing, riding steadily southward toward Beatty. While the world slept, he was fully awake, feeling confident and strong and free. He took a deep, sweet breath. In this world there was only one vice, only one crime, only one sin — failure. You could be anyone you desired to be; you could do anything you wanted to do, but you could not fail, for the good and orderly people of this world respected only success and they despised only failure. Well, sometimes it took a man ten, maybe fifteen years to learn this, but once learned it was not a lesson a bitter man readily forgot. Promise anything, say anything, be anything, only just don't fail!

His horse's hoofs scuffed up pale moonlighted dust; each iron footfall had a separate echo in the stillness of the roadway. The wide, straight roadway narrowed a little as it entered town, but continued to flow southward through Beatty and out as far as the eye could see, southward. He dismounted at the livery barn and tied up at the hitch rail. Then he leaned there, gazing at the town. At the Royal Antler Saloon, at the Cowmen's & Drovers' Bank, at the Beatty Mercantile Company store front, at the Hereford County Sheriff's Office, at the Queens & Aces Café, at the Beatty Hotel, and the Hereford County Abstract Office — Land Sales Our Specialty. And finally he gazed longest at the square brick courthouse.

Twelve years ago, he thought, *a barefoot kid walked north out of this town in the middle of the night. And now he's back. Fine, that's the way it should be. Judge . . . you sleep good tonight, hear? And you, too, Sheriff. And the rest of you good, substantial citizens . . . you well-fed sanctimonious buzzards . . . you all sleep good tonight, you hear? Because Tom Barker is back and from this night on you're not going to sleep so good . . . any of you!*

II

"Get up, damn you! Get outen them blankets, you dirty little . . . !"

It was late in the night and his head rang from the first blow. He leaped up — and fell, tangled in the bedding. He rolled away from the arcing boot of his father, wide awake in mind but still sluggish in body, terribly frightened but wide-awake.

"I'm awake, Paw. I'm up. . . ."

The arm had clubbed downward again, striking hard.

"Please, Paw, I'm up. I'm up."

"Yes, you're up, you sneakin' little snake, an' you helped her, didn't you?"

The arm was rising again.

"No, Paw, I didn't help anyone. Honest I didn't."

The arm descended again, and that time the boy's knees went soft. Something warm ran down his cheek from an ear.

"Where is she, damn you?"

"Who, Paw?"

The man's wildness remained but its first force was spent. He stood there in the lean-to, reeling like a tree in a high wind, his beard awry, his face shiny with sweat, and his black eyes burning with an endless cruelty and hatred. "Your maw, that's who.

Don't lie to me, damn you. You helped her, didn't you? Who did she go with? Where did they go?"

"Honest, Paw, I don't know."

"Oh, don't you, now!"

The man moved forward, his arm rising. He was a massive person, a freighter by trade. His strength and harshness were famous as far away as Chihuahua. The boy quailed, giving ground, sick in his stomach with fear. One blow felled him, lifted him bodily, and hurled him against the wall, and left him crumpled, white nightshirt spotted with blood.

Later, with the night as quiet as death, the boy had stirred, sat up, seen that his father was gone, and had gone out to the well to wash his face and daub at his torn ear, swollen as large as his fist. And then he had heard the man coming along the road roaring drunk, had run back for his clothes, put them on in panting haste, and had fled into the night without his shoes.

First, he had hidden at Grogan's Livery Barn, but the night hawk had run him off. Later, after sunup, he had begged Moses Beach to let him work for his meals and hide in the store until his father went south with the wagons again. But Beach had also run him off. Then his father had come searching and in terror he had gone to Judge Montgomery, ashamed that Antoinette should see his swollen, purple face, the blood on his clothing, and the terror in his eyes. Portly Judge Montgomery had taken him to Sheriff Tim Pollard and there at the jailhouse, when his father had come in red-eyed and reeling, he had been handed over.

He had never been able to recall accurately what had followed. He remembered being knocked down twice before they had gotten home, but beyond that he knew nothing at all until, after nightfall, he had found himself lying in the yard with his father's drover's whip in the roiled dust beside him, its shot-loaded handle less than ten inches from his head. And that was the night he had left Beatty, sore outside and sick inside, walking barefoot northward.

Then had come the long years between when he had wandered among rough towns and hard men, growing larger, taller, hard-muscled, and as agile as a cat, becoming the deceptively calm-eyed and soft-spoken man he now was. And through those years he had never ceased to cherish the memory of a beautiful woman with dark-red hair, a sad mouth, and gentle blue eyes who had deserted her husband and abandoned her son.

Many a night, with his body turning soft against the hard ground, he had smoked and watched night come on, each silver star a tear, each reddening rampart a wealth of auburn hair, each sighing breeze a smile, letting memory and longing work their sad magic in the one soft spot that remained to him. What had become of her? Who was that man? Of course he had been the one, but it had taken years for the boy to understand this. All he knew, then, before she had left, was that during those long months when his father was away with the wagons, that a man would come to the house, would call for her in a top buggy, would bring her presents from St. Louis or St. Joe.

He had been a middle-size man with a constant, big-toothed smile and a way of looking from beneath his lashes that had been cultivated. And he was a soft-spoken man with a gentle air, and that, too, had been part of his cultivated personality. Did she, even yet, in her new life, think of the little boy back in Beatty? Yes, she would remember him. A mother couldn't ever forget.

He could visualize her very clearly sitting somewhere combing her hair with silver-backed brushes; they had initials engraved on them but he could not make them out, and the room she was in was a fine one. It had flowery paper on the walls and a thick carpet underfoot. It was somewhere in the East, maybe in St. Louis, or maybe even farther East, maybe in Chicago or Cincinnati or New York. In his sadness he had always been glad for her. He had only wished he might have been with her. But he couldn't, although he had never permitted himself to believe she hadn't wanted him with her. It was the man with the false smile; he had not wanted her son to be with her. He had wanted her for himself alone.

Also during those years he had heard of his father. Down along the border and over into New Mexico — even as far south as Chihuahua — there were tales of terrible drunks, savage fights, legends of bitterness, of cruelty, and unrestrained ferocity. They had left him unmoved. He had never doubted that he and his father would one day meet again face to face, but this plausibility had long since ceased to mean anything to him. He had neither pity nor hatred for the man. He thought of him only as a failure, a man who goaded oxen and mule trains, a laborer, a drover who sweated and froze and fought to deliver the goods of others. He remembered the beatings and cursings, but only distantly and vaguely; they might have happened to someone else. He rarely thought of the man at all, and, when he did, it was simply to measure him by the same yardstick he measured all men with — success or failure. Beyond that his father might have been dead — or as vanished as his mother — or as meaningless and distant as all those departed yesterdays. With the exception of the one memory, the past was past and he did not mean for it to influence him in the future, beyond putting to practice the lessons it had taught him.

Now, standing in the paling light of a new day, smoking and watching the town, he could afford a small smile. The lessons he had learned were practical ones. The hand dangling above his gun holstered at his hip, for instance, was very experienced. The dark eyes, beguilingly gentle, were all-seeing. The naturally dark face, further colored by Arizona's fierce sun, hid all emotion behind its smoothness, its blank, almost melancholy expression. Only the square jaw, thin lip line, and molded thrust of chin offered any clue of the inner man Tom Barker had become.

III

Judge Montgomery remembered hearing what had sounded to him like a shot. But he had been busy at the courthouse, and, since no one had mentioned it, he had forgotten about it until, upon arriving home in the warm brightness of a long summer evening, he found Sheriff Tim Pollard on the porch with his daughter. The judge was a stout man with a handsome head and thick gray hair. He looked every inch a judge, or a senator, or perhaps an Indian commissioner from Washington. He was a punctual, orderly person whose long tenure of respectability had covered him with layer after layer of decorum. He disliked spontaneity, had never in his life given a snap judgment, and he abhorred raw emotionalism in any of its myriad forms. Violence, rawness, sensationalism in any form was anathema to him, and, because he was this way, the substantial people of Hereford County had returned him to office at every election in the past twenty years.

Judge Montgomery's own life having been an orderly sequence of dignified advancement under the law, he looked upon any other kind of progress as a form of sordidness. He outwardly respected the people of

Hereford County who had won the wilderness from the Indians with guns and scalping knives, but inwardly he disapproved of them strongly. They were crude, savage, dirty people, in his opinion no better than the Indians themselves. Therefore, when he saw Tim Pollard, himself an old Indian fighter, sitting on the porch with Antoinette, his secret antagonism rose up. Besides it was a beautiful evening, he was a little tired, and had been looking forward to relaxing in the soft, silent twilight. He nodded to the sheriff, smiled at Antoinette, touched her shoulder lightly in passing, and sank down upon a chair with a repressed sigh.

"There was a killing in town today, Judge," Pollard said.

Remembering the gunshot sound, Judge Montgomery nodded without speaking. He knew Tim Pollard; the sheriff would tell his story in his own way and in his own good time.

"Charley Ingersoll got it."

Judge Montgomery drew up in his chair. Ingersoll was one of the more prominent settlers. He was an industrious man, a hard worker, violent tempered perhaps, but substantial, and a man with a good bank balance. Anger slowly built up in the judge. "Tim, we've got to do something about those cowboys. I've been telling you for years there's got to be an ordinance against carrying pistols in town."

"It wasn't the cowmen this time, Judge."

"No? Then who?"

Tim Pollard ran the back of one freckled hand under his drooping longhorn mustache; he squinted toward the faraway hills where the sun was fast disappearing. He pushed long legs out in front of him and regarded the scuffed toes of his boots.

"Well?" the judge said impatiently.

"You recollect Tom Barker's kid?"

"His kid?"

"Yeah. Think back, Judge. You recollect how Tom's wife run off one night, and old Tom went around town like a crazy man for a couple days afterward?"

"I recall that," Judge Montgomery said shortly, finding the subject sordid and therefore unpleasant, particularly so in front of his daughter.

"Recollect young Tom . . . the kid . . . hidin' from old Tom and tryin' to get folks to keep the old man away from him?"

"*Hmmmmm,* vaguely, Tim."

Pollard turned a long, thoughtful gaze on the judge. "He went to you an' you brought him to me."

"Well, what of it?"

"And I turned him over to his old man."

The judge was frowning. "I remember now," he said. "It was back a few years."

Antoinette spoke for the first time. "It was over ten years ago." She was watching her father now. "He ran away that same night."

Sheriff Pollard nodded slowly. "That's right. He run off that night and no one ever heard of him again. Well, Judge . . . he's back. It was young Tom Barker who killed Charley Ingersoll today."

The judge digested this in silence. He could not place the boy's face at all; he remembered only the general details of that earlier sordidness, and, since he had no respect at all for the elder Tom Barker, he found it easy to extend this antipathy to the returned son. "Did you arrest him?" he now asked the sheriff.

"No."

"No? Well, why not, Tim?"

"Charley was beatin' his horse at the emporium hitch rail, Judge. He was usin' a pick handle. Young Barker walked up, knocked Charley down, took up the pick handle, and worked him over a mite with it." Pollard's words fell quietly, slowly into the soft glow of dying day. He was squinting far out again, and obviously his mind was reliving the events of another decade.

"Well, Charley commenced to get up. Young Barker stood back. Charley went for his gun under his coat and quicker'n scat young Tom killed him." The sheriff was looking steadily now at Antoinette. "It was a fair fight, Judge. Ingersoll was killed going for his gun."

"Witnesses?" the judge asked mechanically.

"Four."

"I see. And I suppose they were Barker's friends."

"Nope, not a one of 'em knew him."

"Correction, Sheriff," Antoinette said. "One of them did."

Pollard's blank face puckered into the smallest of rueful smiles. "Excuse me, Toni." He shifted his gaze to the judge. "One of 'em recognized him right off as young Tom Barker. She was the only one who did, though."

"She?" Judge Montgomery said, then, with understanding coming, he looked incredulously at his daughter. "You, honey?"

Antoinette nodded.

"But what were you doing . . . why, you might have been hurt?" Judge Montgomery's face reddened. "Tim, confound it, I'm going to insist on a special meeting of the town council. Now, tonight, we're going to pass that no guns ordinance."

Pollard was tugging at his mustache. He said: "It'll be a good thing, all right, Judge. Only I think there's something else ought to be tended to first."

"What? What can possibly be more important . . . ?"

"Young Tom Barker."

Judge Montgomery fixed angry eyes on the sheriff. He had known Tim Pollard many years; the sheriff was a dry and laconic man; he emphasized his opinions with a minimum number of words. "Elaborate, Tim. What about young Barker?"

"Judge, I've seen a heap of gunmen in my time. I don't mean just the fast guns, either . . . I mean the kind of men who use guns to serve their private ends. That's the kind of a killer young Tom Barker is."

"I don't follow you, Tim."

"A killer rides into town, Judge. He shoots someone, collects his five hundred dollars, and rides on to the next town. That's the kind of gunman most of us are familiar with. But in the past few years another kind of gunman has come along. The Wyatt Earp kind. They don't kill just for the five hundred. They don't kill for hire at all. They use their guns to get something they particularly want, something like wealth or position. That's the kind of a gunman young Tom Barker is. He's in Beatty for a good reason."

Judge Montgomery settled back in his chair. He, too, turned his gaze outward toward the marching ranks of shadows moving down the distant hills. He said quietly: "I take it you talked to him."

"I did."

"What did he say?"

"Nothing. He offered to surrender his gun. Told me why he shot Charley Ingersoll. That's all."

"Did you ask him why he came back?"

"Yup. He said it wasn't any of my business . . . which it wasn't."

"Then what makes you leery of him, Tim?"

"A feelin' I've got, Judge. Like I said, I've seen a heap of gunmen in my time. Young Tom's not in Beatty to look up any old friends because he's got none here. He's here for a good reason and he aims to stay until he's worked it out."

A long interval of silence descended. Antoinette finally arose. "I'll get you both some lemonade," she said. "Mister Beach got a fresh load of Sonora lemons in today."

After she was gone, the judge settled deeper into his chair, sighed, put both hands palms down on his paunch, and let his eyelids droop. He felt resigned, remote, pleasantly loose. "If Ingersoll's killing was justifiable homicide, Tim," he murmured, "I suppose that's that. But I'm still going to push for the town ordinance against firearms."

"The ordinance will help," Sheriff Pollard replied, bending forward to make a cigarette. "But that doesn't solve the Barker problem. He'll kill again, Judge."

"Who?"

Pollard shrugged. "How would I know? I just know that he will. He's in Beatty for a damned good reason, Judge. The first one of us who gets in his way will get called out."

"Well, what do you suggest? We can't just run him out of town. He has his legal rights."

"I got nothing to suggest. I just wanted you to know that your gun ordinance all of a sudden ain't so important to me any more."

"You're barking up a tree, Tim. The boy has a bad background. He won't stay long in a place as quiet and orderly as Beatty."

Sheriff Pollard lit his cigarette, smoked it a moment in silence, then grunted. As far as he was concerned the conversation was ended, and it had run just about as he had expected it to. Judge Montgomery was a good man for the town, and on the bench, but he'd never, in Pollard's opinion, been much of a man in a lot of other ways.

IV

Under a hot pink brightness Tom Barker stirred in his blankets, raised up, and propped his head on one hand, gazing along the pearl-gray floor of desert, misty and silent, until the land lifted and met the sharp edge of the rising sun. It was after 5:00, daylight was coming, and it would be another scorching summer day. While he watched, the first dazzling rays shot above the distant hills, raced across the desert, and struck with quick brightness the warped roofs of the little town down on the plain that he had left the night before to go up into the hills and camp. Nearby were the graceful willows in a narrow arroyo, dim and gray, still holding the dregs of the night; they lined an unseen stream that tinkled pleasantly in the hush. He yawned, spat, pushed back the blanket, and sat up. Down along the creek fetlock-deep in yellow forage grass his horse stamped and blew its nose.

Tom scrubbed at the creek, hustled twigs

for a breakfast fire, and worked silently with the fat, rich aroma of frying side meat rising into the air. He was rocking the iron fry pan gently when a laughing voice drawled behind him, back in the tangled willows.

"If I was a sheriff, you'd never live to eat that, Tom."

Barker made no move. He rocked the pan gently over its arrow points of blue fire, his averted face turning handsome under the influence of a dry small smile. "If you were a sheriff, I'd have roped and tied you when you scuffed that rock with your spur ten minutes ago."

The newcomer straightened up and came out of the willows. He was as tall as Barker but not nearly as broad. An air of litheness preceded him; he walked like an Indian, balancing forward on the balls of his feet. Beneath his hat a tawny lock of sun-rusted dark hair hung upon his forehead. His face was youthful, burned brown, and prematurely lined. He squatted next to Barker, watching the faint gray smoke rise up, then curve away and hang in the arroyo to mingle with the shadowy vestiges of night.

"I'm hungrier'n a bitch wolf," the newcomer said, watching the bacon curl. "You know . . . that's quite a ride in one day and one night, Tom."

"I'll feed you and I'll pay you," Tom replied without looking away from the fry pan, "but damned if I'll sympathize with you, Tex."

A strong, boyish ripple of laughter came from Tex. His eyes crinkled and danced. "That's good enough," he said. "Just feed me first . . . then tell me what this is all about."

Tom divided the side meat into two rations and settled back. "Eat," he said, and for a moment added nothing to it. "I won't tell you why I'm doing this Tex. All I'll tell you is what you're to do."

"Suits me, Tom. Shoot."

"See that little town down there?"

"Yup. Saw it before sunup."

"That's Beatty."

"All right."

"I'm going to make it or break it."

Tex paused to look across the dying fire. He did not speak; he only shrugged, then returned to eating.

"I'm going to be top lash in that town. I'm going to tell the sheriff who to arrest and who to leave alone. I'm going to call a tune and the judge's going to dance to it. I'm going to buy and sell a feller named Moses Beach . . . and you're going to help me do it."

Tex put the fry pan down and wiped his fingers along the seams of his worn trousers. He reached for his tobacco sack, frowned over a cigarette, lit it with a twig from the fire, exhaled mightily, then leaned back and gazed steadily at Tom Barker from fearless, hard blue eyes. "You know I ain't a questioning man, Tom. We've shared too many bedrolls an' cook fires an' roundups an' drunks not to know one another pretty well."

"That's right."

"I'm not a killer, Tom."

Barker scoured the fry pan with dry grass and dust. He worked hard at it, frowning, lips flattened in a bleak line. "I don't need a killer, Tex. All I need is a man who'll do what I say. Any killing's got to be done . . . I'll do it."

"You don't understand me, Tom. I don't want to tie up with a killer, either."

Barker's head came up slowly. "You think I'm a killer, Tex?"

Tex thumbed back his hat; the heavy dark curl spread more fully across his forehead. His face creased slightly. "Tom," he said slowly, "you're plumb capable of becoming a killer. Years back, I figured there was something inside you that was pretty twisted. Like I said, fellers get to know one another pretty well when they pardner up and face all sorts of situations together. Also, like I said, I ain't a questioning man. I always thought the world of you, Tom . . . but I've always known there was something inside you, too . . . I just never questioned what it was or why it was there."

Tom turned away to push the fry pan into a saddlebag. He spoke while his head was averted. His voice sounded deep and gentle when next he spoke. "I killed a man yesterday, Tex. He was beating a horse with a pick handle. There was blood running out of the critter's nose."

Tex nodded understanding and approval, but the speculative expression did not leave his face. "All right. That's no crime. But that ain't what I'm talking about, either, and you know it."

"There'll be no unnecessary killing, Tex."

A space of solemn silence settled around the guttering cook fire. Finally Tex killed his cigarette and regarded its broken, brown form in the bent-flat grass. "All right, Tom. We understand one another. What am I to do?"

Barker reached inside his shirt, brought forth a thick packet of oilskin, unwrapped it gently, and withdrew a $100 bill from the thick sheaf of green paper. "Take this and spend it at the Royal Antler Saloon. Listen to everything that's said. Twice a week we'll meet up here, on Mondays and Fridays."

"Listen for what, Tom?"

"Gossip. Who is buying whose cattle, who is in need of a jag of hay, who's borrowing money at the bank. Stuff like that."

"Just local gossip? Tom, you sure you know what you're doing?"

Barker grinned. "If I don't, the worst thing that'll happen is that we'll ride out of this country like we rode in . . . quietly."

Tex folded the $100 bill thoughtfully. "Must've been a lot of loot on that stage," he said, arising.

Tom's grin lingered. "Maybe there was. Only I didn't get it. I saved that money . . . been saving it for years."

"Uhn-huh. One more thing, Tom. I don't know you?"

"That's right. You're a stranger. You're just riding through. You're resting your horse. You've been on a long drive, been paid off, and aren't in any hurry about hunting up a new job."

"All right," Tex said, gazing along the perimeter of hills, then lowering his eyes suddenly to Beatty. "It's your money and your play. I'll be here come Friday."

■ ■ ■ ■

Tom did nothing for half an hour after Tex departed. He smoked beside the dead fire, narrowed his eyes against the fierce sun smash, and gazed steadily down at Beatty. Then he caught his horse, saddled and bridled, stepped across the saddle, and swung out across the hills southwesterly so that, when he rode into town shortly before high noon, he came in from the south.

He paid for a room overlooking the town at the Beatty Hotel, one month in advance, then he hired a boy to haul water for a tub in the lean-to bathhouse, and soaked. Afterward, freshly dressed, his thick hair shiny with oil and his ivory-butted gun lashed down and moving rhythmically with each step, he went to the Royal Antler, took a wall table, and called for a drink. There he sat, low and loose with his back to the wall, feeling the full run of confidence; he had waited a long time; now he was back. One slip, one error, could spoil it all. He would make no mistakes; his impatience was under an iron leash. This chance would never in his lifetime come again. And yet, in spite of the hot willfulness in his mind, this sitting here was a form of release, too. It was a nearing of the end of the trail. It was the kind of release a man like Tom Barker had to have. The years had built up too much inside of him. Some way, all of this was going to come out fiercely, in a drunk, a fight, or a kiss.

The second whiskey made him hungry. He moved to the food table, spooned chili into a bowl, slapped a fat slice of Sonora onion between two dark slabs of bread, and took the meal back to his table. For a man who had been hungry for days on end many times in his life, food was both a reward and a luxury. It was a deep comfort to be eating, freshly bathed and dressed, in Beatty's finest saloon, listening to the ebb and flow of talk, the sharp slap of booted feet and the soft ring of spurs. His presence here was in a sense a personal triumph and he savored it.

Later, smoking a cigar, studying the range men, the townsmen, travelers, and drifters, drawing in the smoke with keen relish, he considered the room with thoughtful complacency. This was one of those rare times in a man's life when the little things that meant so much gave him his greatest moments: cold spring water on a scorching day; the powerful softening of his body against the earth after a punishing ride; the biting flavor of a cigar after months of abstinence; returning to the town that had ignored a boy's breaking heart, knowing this time the town would never forget him. These were the simple, gratifying things of life, things that went down deep into a man. But none of them were free. A man earned them by sweat and hunger, by privation and fatigue, so in the end that was why they were good.

He saw the tall, loose body come through the door, hesitate, cross his blank dark stare with its moving blue glance, then proceed to the bar and lean there, elbows extended, long legs knee-sprung in total relaxation, and he smiled to himself. Tex Earle was a fine actor, as good perhaps as Wilkes Booth himself, and now there was no further need for him to linger. He arose, left a coin on the table, and crossed the room to pass out into the warm night beyond.

Beatty was drenched in blackness. It dripped on him from roof tops and curdled the orange glow from windows. It was a formless substance that smothered everything except movement, and, because it did, he did not see the rangy silhouette even after he had passed it by. Then a voice, softly commanding, struck him in the back.

"Barker. Just a minute."

He recognized the voice even as he turned.

He remembered it from his last day in Beatty as a youth. The yellow-stained light of a saloon window ran sickly across the older man's path as he approached, and for a moment Tom could not see above it.

"It's Pollard, Barker. Tim Pollard." The sheriff stepped across the yellow dust and peered ahead. His raw-boned appearance was accentuated by the night. When next he spoke, his voice was crowded with thoughtfulness. "Figured we might talk a little."

Tom remained motionless and silent, separating the man from the night.

"I got a notion about yesterday's killing," Pollard said.

"Have you?"

"Yeah. I figure you could have kicked the gun out of Ingersoll's hand. Or maybe knocked him out with that pick handle. I don't figure you had to kill him."

"Didn't I?"

"No. I've disarmed a lot of men, Barker. When you're standing less than six feet from 'em, it's no chore."

"Then why did I kill him?"

Pollard slumped, resting all his weight on one leg. Before replying he ran a hand under his heavy mustache. "Because you wanted to."

"I didn't know the man."

"You didn't have to, Barker. You were cocked and primed to kill someone. Ingersoll gave you a plumb fine excuse."

"You make it sound like murder, Sheriff."

"I wish I could prove it was, Barker."

"Why? You scarcely remember me."

"Well," Pollard said slowly, picking his words, "you got no reason to like this town. I understand that. Sometimes a feller gets something like that fixed in his head and packs it around with him for years. Sometimes he gets a chance to come back and cut a swathe. Sort of make the town get down on its knees to him. I think that's what's wrong with you. Why else would you come back here? You got no friends here. Your folks . . . well, I reckon you understand about them."

Barker's voice turned husky. "No, Sheriff," he said, "tell me about them."

But Tim Pollard recognized the signs and simply wagged his head. "I can't say it the way it should be said, so I'd best not say it at all. But you understand me all right, Barker."

Tom ground his heels down into the dust of the plank walk. "You talk too much, old man," he said coldly. "Talk too much and do too little. You're not the only one in Beatty who's been eating too regularly for too many years."

"So?"

Tom Barker's jaw snapped closed. He continued to regard the sheriff a moment longer, then turned on his heel and went along the plank walk as far as the hotel. There, he turned in without a backward glance.

Sheriff Pollard made a cigarette, lit it, leaning against a post, and smoked in thoughtful silence until a short, ugly man came up beside him and stopped.

"Beautiful night, Tim."

Pollard grunted. "Moses, us old-timers've had it pretty good in the valley for a long time, haven't we?"

Moses Beach looked up with a scowl. "Sure. What of it? We settled this damned country, didn't we? We made 'er what she is, didn't we? Then we're entitled to a reward, aren't we?"

"Maybe," the sheriff answered, gazing up the darkened road. "But maybe we've taken too much for granted these past ten or twelve years, Moses."

"What the hell are you talkin' about?"

"That killin' yesterday . . . and the feller who did it."

"Young Barker? Is he still around? I

thought he'd hightail it when you let him go."

"I never had him, an' he didn't hightail it."

Beach puffed a moment on his cigar, following the direction of Pollard's gaze. "Too bad he had to pick Ingersoll," he said finally. "Charlie was a good account."

The sheriff made a mirthless smile. "He was also a human bein', Moses. That's what I mean about us old-timers havin' things too easy these past years." He threw down his cigarette and stamped it hard. "Beatty's due for a jolt, I think."

"What d'you mean . . . a jolt?"

Pollard straightened up. "Just what I said . . . a jolt. Good night, Moses."

Beach's small eyes regarded the sheriff's retreating back until it disappeared into the night, then he turned and struck off in the opposite direction.

V

Tom Barker had been three weeks in Beatty before he made a move, and of course by the end of that time everyone knew who he was. Mostly they addressed him as Mr. Barker. What the cowmen and merchants and townsmen did not know was that Tom Barker knew as much about them as they knew about themselves. No one had as yet associated the blue-eyed Texan who hung out at the Royal Antler Saloon with the black-eyed man who, rumor said, had had a drunk for a father and whose mother had run off with another man years before. Folks had, after the fashion of people, weighed and measured Tom Barker, had decided he was a gunman, and accorded him all the respect that appellation inspired, but socially they had nothing to do with him. Still, after three weeks of obvious inactivity even Sheriff Pollard was beginning to have doubts about his earlier suspicions. It did not seem reasonable that a man like dark Tom Barker would sit around day after day, if he had anything sinister in mind, or if he had anything better to do.

Then, when Tom finally struck, no one at first associated the action with Mr. Barker who spent his time between the Royal Antler Saloon and the Beatty Hotel, and had never once set his foot inside Beatty's bank, where rancher Gerald Finnerty and banker Elihu Gorman faced one another across Gorman's desk.

"The receipt," Finnerty was saying, enjoying Gorman's discomfort very much, even smiling openly at it, "the receipt, Elihu."

"That's a lot of money," the banker murmured, his gaze fixed to the pile of bills on his desk. "Couldn't you use it to better advantage restocking or expanding, Gerald?"

"I could," Finnerty assented. "Only I'd rather have my note back. The receipt, please, Elihu."

"Where did you get it, Gerald?" the banker asked, making no motion to take up his pen.

Finnerty colored; his eyes turned hard as flint. "Well, now," he said coldly, "I don't figure that's any of your business . . . where I come by that money."

Gorman picked up his pen and began to write. Beyond the glassed-in cubicle of his office there was the subdued sound of talk, the sigh of movement, the swish of clothing. Inside the cubicle there was only the scratching of Gorman's pen upon the paper. When he put the pen aside, Gerald Finnerty reached forward, took up the paper, and scrutinized it. Then he folded it very carefully and put it into his pocket, and the smile returned to his face.

"One thing more. When the note's receipted at the courthouse, mail it to me."

"Yes, of course."

Gorman pushed himself upright again. He looked physically uncomfortable and his voice sounded weak. "If you extended the loan . . . which the bank'd be glad to do for you . . . then you could buy out the Miller place and really expand."

"I can buy out the Miller place anyway," Finnerty said shortly, taking up his hat and turning toward the door. "In fact, I took a cash option on it day before yesterday."

Elihu Gorman remained standing for several minutes after Finnerty left, then he went as far as the door and called to a clerk. "Go get Mister Beach," he ordered, closed the door, returned to his chair, and sat down to wait.

When Moses Beach came into Gorman's office, he looked annoyed. It was early in the day and most people, wishing to avoid the heat, did their shopping early. "What is it?" he demanded shortly.

"Finnerty was just in here. He paid off his note." Gorman nodded toward the crumpled money on his desk.

Beach moved closer. "In full?"

"In full and I gave him a receipt. I had to."

Beach stood a moment, then retreated to a chair and dropped down. "How?" he asked as the annoyance vanished from his face. "He had his back to the wall."

"I don't know how."

"What d'you mean . . . you don't know?"

The banker's face darkened; his voice got sharp. "What difference does it make how he got the money, dammit. There it is. His loan is paid off. We can't make the deal with Houston. And . . . we're committed to pay off that thirty percent money we borrowed for three months, which we figured to buy the Finnerty place from the bank with after it'd foreclosed."

"I want to know where he got that money," Beach said, his face gone white beneath lowered brows. "Maybe he stole it, robbed a stage or something."

Gorman's irritation increased. There was perspiration on his forehead and upper lip. "You fool, Moses," he snapped. "The money's not important right now. What if he did steal it? We've still got to honor the note."

Beach made an agitated gesture toward the frosted glass partition. "You want the whole world to know?" he demanded. "Lower your voice."

Gorman subsided, threw himself back into his chair, and remained silent.

"How do we get out of this, now?" the storekeeper asked.

"We don't."

"There's got to be a way, Elihu."

"Sure, we pay off like we agreed to do . . .

in three months at thirty percent interest."

"No!"

"Yes! We've been building up the value of the Finnerty place to Evan Houston for a year now. We even justified our own borrowing by making that loan on the false appraisal."

"Damn it, I know all that."

"Sure you do. You also know Houston is ready to buy, too, and that the bank was set to foreclose this month, and on the strength of that . . . and my position here . . . you and I borrowed forty thousand to redeem the place from the bank. Now, Moses, you take your copy of that loan paper to Phoenix and ask any lawyer down there how you get out of repaying . . . and he'll tell you that you don't get out of it, that you repay."

Beach wiped his face with a sleeve and continued to stare at Gorman. "There's got to be a way, Elihu," he said huskily.

"I don't know what it is. While I was waiting for you, I did some thinking."

"Go on."

"Suppose Houston goes to Finnerty now?"

"Well, what if he does?"

"Finnerty'll sell to him."

Beach's eyes widened with comprehension. "After we've built Houston up on the value and Finnerty'll get the profit . . . ?"

"That's right."

After a moment of agonized silence Moses Beach got to his feet and crossed to the door. "I got to get back," he husked. "I'll see you tonight, Elihu. We got to think of something . . . something. . . ."

Gorman also arose. "When you gamble big," he intoned, "you win big or you lose big. All right. I'll be here at the bank after closing time."

Moses Beach stopped on the plank walk in front of the bank, gulping big lungfuls of insufficient oxygen. It was difficult to breathe. When people passed, some nodding, some speaking, he ignored them. Riders and buggies and battered ranch wagons ground through the roadway's dust; he scarcely saw them. Opposite him in the shade of the Royal Antler's overhang, two talking men caught and retained his attention. One of them was broadly smiling. Moses recognized him instantly as cowman Gerald Finnerty. The other man, hawk-like in profile, dark and thoughtful-looking, was Tom Barker. Very gradually suspicion began to form in Moses Beach's mind.

Barker and Finnerty passed from sight through the saloon doorway. They were going to have a drink together, going to celebrate. Beach's eyes turned glassy; a haziness obscured things. He put out a hand, grasped an upright, and steadied himself. How? How had Barker found out? Why did he give Finnerty the money? What was he doing? What was he up to?

When the dizziness momentarily lessened, Moses crossed the road. Gorman had said it didn't matter where the money had come from; the important thing was that Finnerty had redeemed his note. Moses grimaced. The important thing wasn't Finnerty or his note at all; it was the $40,000 repayable within ninety days at thirty percent interest.

As the day wore on, Beach's trouble getting enough oxygen increased and he went home at 3:30 in the afternoon. At 6:00, while Elihu Gorman was consulting his watch impatiently, Dr. Albigence Spence was informing Moses Beach's wife that her husband had suffered a severe stroke and would be bedridden for weeks, and might even be permanently paralyzed.

At 6:30 Dr. Spence left the Beach residence, went to the Royal Antler for his nightcap, met Judge Montgomery there on his way home from the courthouse, and told him what had happened. The judge was aghast; so was the lanky blue-eyed cowboy lounging beside him at the bar.

"But he's not an old man," the judge said, looking down upon the medical man's less majestic height. "He's no older than you or me, Al."

Dr. Spence drank off his sour mash and nodded for another. "Since when's age got anything to do with a stroke?" he asked absently, watching the bartender's hands.

"Well, I don't know, but. . . ."

"You're pale as a ghost, Judge. Have a refill on me."

The judge had his second drink; color returned to his face; his voice firmed up. "What caused it?" he asked.

Dr. Spence turned irritable. "How the hell would I know? All I know is that he had it."

"Will he recover all right?"

"Who knows? He'll never be the same again, I can tell you that. My guess is that there's damage to his brain. How much damage, or to what extent he'll recover from it, I have no idea. Only time can answer that."

The doctor was turning away. Judge Montgomery put out a hand. "What did he say?"

"Nothing. They don't talk, Judge. Cerebral hemorrhages don't ordinarily occur or continue to occur during consciousness. He's unconscious. In fact, he may not even know anything's happened to him for several days."

The doctor started forward again, then stopped as a tall, erect man, looking disgruntled and testy, came up, nodded, and motioned for a drink.

" 'Evening, Judge. 'Evening, Doctor."

Spence bobbed his head. "Just came from Moses's place, Elihu. He's had a stroke."

The tall man stiffened; his hand, extended for the shot glass, grew still on the bar top. "A stroke?"

"Yes." Spence looked from Judge Montgomery to the banker. His voice sounded dry now. "You'd better drink that. I don't want any more patients tonight."

Elihu Gorman drank and set the glass down. "Is he dead?"

"No, he's alive. But he's not out of the woods by a damned sight."

"I need another drink," Gorman said, and abruptly turned his back on the room, bending forward over the bar.

Dr. Spence frowned, nodded to the judge, and left. The lanky cowboy beside Montgomery had both elbows on the bar. He was nursing an amber glass of ale in both hands and looking steadily into the backbar mirror. Visible to him against the north wall, lounging there with a bottle, a glass, and a bowl of chili was Tom Barker. From time to time the dark man would gaze at the banker and at the judge, then he would sip his whiskey. The lighting was poor except in the center of the room and Barker's face was obscure. The Texan drank his ale a little at a time. He was wondering how much revenge Tom wanted from this little town.

VI

Moses Beach regained consciousness the day following his stroke, but Albigence Spence's prognosis had been correct; there was brain damage. There was also a partial paralysis that prevented Beach from using his hands, arms, or vocal cords. He lay like a vegetable in his bed, alive and physically functioning, but in all other respects quite dead. Dr. Spence called often; it was an interesting case. He had no great feeling for Beach, he had known him too long for that, but it was an interesting case. One rarely found real medical challenges on the frontier. What particularly intrigued Spence was the extent of brain damage, and when, if Beach recovered, he would be normal again. Spence rather doubted it. Another thing that interested him was the odd attitude of Elihu Gorman since Beach's stroke. Gorman was drinking more lately and he was so preoccupied most of the time that he scarcely recognized lifelong acquaintances.

Dr. Spence knew, as did everyone else around Beatty, that Beach and Gorman were allies in any number of financial ventures, that they held whip hands over most of the cowmen and some of the merchants. He could easily surmise, then, that Beach's stroke affected in some way their financial partnership and Gorman was worried over it. The extent of Gorman's anxiety was plain in his actions. Dr. Spence found this amusing because he held Elihu Gorman in as scornful a light as he did Moses Beach. In fact, it cheered him, which was a vast improvement because his normal disposition was cynical and generally brusque.

Two other men were affected by Beach's illness. Tom Barker met Tex Earle at the creek overlooking Beatty on a blistering Friday afternoon. They smoked and talked and sat cross-legged in the shade, Indian-like, through intervals of long silence, each busy with his thoughts. Tex whittled a twig with long, smooth sweeps of his Barlow knife and puffed desultorily upon a cigarette dangling from his lips. "You know who owns half the livery barn, don't you?" he said.

Barker shook his head. "No. Who?"

"The judge."

"And . . . ?"

"And the barn gets its hay and grain from Finnerty. Has for years."

Tom's dark face hosted a faint smile. "Fine. The price of hay and grain just went up."

Tex continued to whittle. "They'll get it somewhere else."

"Where?"

"I don't know."

"Find out."

Tex regarded his stick through squinted eyes. "You'll run out of money, Tom. You can't buy every cowman in the valley."

"No, but I can option all their hay and grain."

"Huh?"

"Pay 'em a little money to tie up their crops for, say, sixty days. If I don't pay the rest, they keep my money. If I do pay 'em the rest . . . the grain and hay are mine."

"Oh, that's what's called an option, eh?"

"Yeah."

Tex lowered his head; shavings fell in long pale curls under his knife. "But it's still a losing proposition. You're still going to lose your money."

Tom made a cigarette and lit it before he replied. "Maybe," he conceded. "And maybe not. Finnerty's making up a drive of fat two-year olds for the San Carlos Agency. He's going to pay me off as soon as he gets back. Fifteen percent interest on my money." Tom exhaled and fixed his gaze upon the town below them. "That fifteen percent'll amount to nine months' wages as a rider, Tex." He paused. "I'm beginning to understand how men make money without working for it."

Earle threw the twig away, snapped his knife closed, and pocketed it. "Yeah," he said dryly, getting to his feet. "But they earn it, Tom. Take that storekeeper lying in bed down there and turning purple in the face trying to tell folks things."

Barker's head twisted. "What do you mean?"

"That cantankerous old sawbones. He gets a couple drinks behind his belt and shoots off his mouth like an old squaw. He was telling the sheriff last night that Beach's rational now, and acts like he's about to bust trying to talk."

Barker considered this. It required no vast deductive power to guess what Beach was upset about. Someway, perhaps through Finnerty although the cowman had been sworn to secrecy, Beach knew who had put up the redemption money. He was apparently trying to tell who it was, which meant that Gorman didn't yet know. If Beach did know and Gorman didn't know, then. . . .

Tom got quickly to his feet. Tex covertly eyed him, saw the sharpness of his expression, the hooded knife-edged glitter of his eyes, and let a noiseless sigh pass his lips. He was moving toward his horse when he said: "All you want to know is where else Montgomery'll get the hay?"

"For now, yes."

"See you Monday, then," Tex said, gathering his reins and vaulting into the saddle. "Tom?"

"Yeah?"

"You going to the dance?"

"What dance?"

"Volunteer firemen's dance at the Methodist Church Sunday evening."

Barker started to speak and stopped. He was balancing something in his mind. He shrugged finally and said: "I might at that, Tex. You supposed to fetch a girl along?"

"If you want to, but it ain't the law hereabouts. Me, I'm taking Miss Eloise from the Royal Antler."

"I might see you there."

Tex laughed and the boyishness returned to his face. In a light voice he said: "If you're there, you'll see me all right." Then he rode away.

Tom did not mount immediately, and, when he did, he made the same circuitous ride he ordinarily did after one of their meetings, and loped into Beatty from the south with afternoon shadows running along before him.

At the hotel Sheriff Tim Pollard pushed himself up out of a chair when Tom entered and stopped him on the stairs with a mild greeting.

" 'Evening, Mister Barker."

"Sheriff."

"If you're not too busy, I'd like to have a little talk with you."

"All right," Tom replied. "Talk."

Sheriff Pollard considered this. From the corner of his eye he saw the desk clerk straining to hear. "Might be better in private," he mumbled.

Tom led the way to his upstairs room, kicked a chair forward for Pollard, and crossed to the window, turned and stood with his back to the dying light, legs spread wide and impatience shading his face. "Talk," he said again.

Pollard did not start right away. He studied the powerful shoulders, thick legs, and finally bent his serene gaze upon the handsome, forceful face. "I guess you can take care of yourself, all right," he speculated.

"Leastways you got the look of a man who can."

Tom stood in silence, waiting.

"Charley Ingersoll's brother is comin' for you."

"Is that a fact?" Tom said coldly.

Pollard's eyes narrowed the slightest bit. "It's a fact," he repeated quietly. "Y'know, Barker, you're sure not goin' out of your way to make friends in Beatty."

Tom rocked forward on his toes. "There's a Methodist minister in town, isn't there?"

Pollard nodded, looking a little puzzled.

"Then let him do the preaching, Sheriff."

Pollard flushed and stood up. The deceptive drowsiness was gone now and his voice was hard. "We don't like troublemakers here, Barker."

"But you got no law against a man protecting himself."

"An ordinary man . . . no. A gunfighter . . . yes. We got laws here."

"Sundown laws, Sheriff?"

"That's right. A gunfighter'll get till sundown to leave town."

"I'm not a gunfighter, though."

Sheriff Pollard went to the door, opened it, and stood half in, half out, of the room. "I'm checkin' on that right now, Barker. If I can prove that you are, you'll leave Beatty.

We don't want any more killings here."

Pollard was moving to close the door when Tom's voice stopped him. "One thing you forgot, Sheriff. A man isn't as easy to push around as a kid."

Pollard closed the door and went along the hall and down the stairs with a deep frown. Back in the room Barker remained stiff and straight. His jaws cut hard lines against his cheeks. He turned slowly and gazed down into the roadway. Puddling shadows were thickening there; there was the acrid scent of dust in the air. Across the road lamplight showed from the bank. Slowly bunched muscles slackened and Tom moved toward the door.

Elihu Gorman was standing beside his desk with one hand braced against the cubicle's flimsy wall, shoving his full weight against it, feeling a heedless kind of fury and frustration. He did not at once hear the knocking, nor did he immediately heed it after he heard it. The knocking grew more insistent. Gorman dropped the arm, pulled himself up, and went out through the empty building and flung back the panel. There were caustic words on his tongue and pointless anger in his eyes, but the big, powerfully-built dark man standing there, evil-looking in the orange light, held him silent.

"My name is Barker," the big man said. "I'd like a few words with you."

"The bank is closed!"

Barker's stare hardened; Gorman braced into it.

"I won't take much of your time and you may find it profitable to listen."

Elihu stepped begrudgingly aside. Tom entered and watched the banker lock the door, straighten up, and march to his office.

From behind his desk Gorman nodded curtly, indicating a chair. Barker did not sit down. He said: "I've got forty thousand dollars I want to put out at small interest on long-term loans."

Gorman's stiffness slowly departed. He sank down behind the desk. The sharpness left his voice; it became deep and pleasant. "How long, Mister Barker?"

"A year, two years."

"You want this money to work for you . . . is that it?"

"That's it."

"Well," Elihu said, and smiled. "Three percent interest?"

"I had three percent in mind, yes."

"Would you consider putting it all out in

one loan at three percent on, say, a two-year basis?"

"I had in mind several small loans."

"Oh, well, of course it's your money, but I can tell you frankly . . . in confidence . . . that I have a place for forty thousand on a two-year plan, and I honestly believe I can get you four percent. It's gilt-edged, Mister Barker."

Tom's brow furrowed. "Four percent sounds good," he said.

"It's as good as gold, Mister Barker."

"Well secured?"

"The bank itself will guarantee it."

Tom's expression of concentration deepened. After a moment he said: "I'll sleep on it."

Elihu arose, held the door for Tom, and escorted him to the roadway entrance. "I'll set it up for you," he said, thrusting his hand out. "All the data will be assembled by eleven o'clock."

"I won't be able to make it until later. About three in the afternoon."

Elihu's teeth flashed; he pumped Tom's hand in a close grip. "At three o'clock." He smiled. "Good night."

Tom crossed to the Royal Antler, exchanged glances with Tex, had two quick jolts of Old Hennessy, and departed. At the livery stable he engaged the night hawk in casual conversation, rented a horse, and rode out. It was then slightly after 8:00 P.M. He did not return until after midnight, and again he engaged the hostler in conversation. He finally went to the hotel and retired at 1:45 in the morning.

Saturday the sun rose bitterly yellow and heat poured over the land in dancing waves. Few riders were abroad. Tom did not meet a soul until the afternoon was well along and he was returning to Beatty. Then he crossed trails with Sheriff Pollard and a young deputy named Jack Havestraw. Enormous crescents of sweat darkened the younger man's shirt but Tim Pollard was only slightly flush-faced and red-necked. He reined in beside Tom with curiosity bright in his eyes.

"Poor time o' day to be ridin'," he said probingly. Tom let the words sink into dead silence.

They rode perhaps two miles before Pollard tried again. "Lots of cow country hereabouts. Thinkin' about going into the cattle business?"

Tom swung his head, fixed Sheriff Pollard with a steady gaze, and said: "I guess you didn't turn up anything."

Pollard shifted slightly in the saddle. The

amiability left his voice and he sighed. "I haven't yet but I'm not through, either. Listen, Barker, I usually bend over backward to get along with folks. You're expectin' me to break my back."

"You don't even have to bend for me, Sheriff. Just keep out of my way."

Tom booted the livery horse into a slow lope and rode away. Pollard's deputy looked angry. "Who is he, anyway? Sure disagreeable."

Tim Pollard watched the diminishing figure swerve toward town. "It isn't who he is that bothers me. I know all about that. It's what he's up to that keeps me awake nights."

"Say," young Havestraw said in a rising tone, "isn't that the feller who shot Charley Ingersoll?"

"It is."

"*Humph!* When Clint finds him, your troubles'll be over."

Tim shook his head with hard emphasis. "Don't you go an' bet any money on that," he growled. "Them as saw him outdraw Charley told me they'd never seen a man so fast with his gun." The sheriff spat aside. "Clint Ingersoll's goin' to get himself killed and you mark my words on that."

Far ahead, Tom hauled up finally and

twisted to watch the sheriff and his deputy straggling their way slowly across the shimmering distance. He smiled and his face did not entirely lose its expression of satisfaction until he swung down at the livery stable, handed the reins to the day man, and bent forward to beat dust from his clothing. He took out his watch, gazed at its face, and crossed to the hotel. It was then 3:00. Elihu Gorman would be waiting. Let him wait.

Tom called for the water boy, gave him a quarter, and lay back in a cool, refreshing bath. Later, while he was dressing, he gave the same lad another quarter to go to the bank and tell Elihu Gorman that Mr. Barker had been detained and could not see him until after 5:00. When the youth departed, Tom winked at his reflection in the mirror and descended to the lobby. The clerk smiled wide approval; there was no denying it, Tom Barker was a fine figure of a man. Everything he wore was dark. The only contrasting relief about him was the ivory grip of his sidearm.

He was sitting in the dark corner of the Royal Antler where he always sat, legs outthrust, shoulders slumped, gazing at the blunt ends of his fingers feeling clean and loose and satisfied, when the night hawk from the livery stable shuffled up. Without a word passing between them, Tom counted out $20 and handed them over. The hostler faced toward the bar with his thirst showing.

A tousle-headed cowboy facing Barker's corner from his place at the poker table saw this transaction over the edge of his cards. His eyes followed the hostler to the bar, watched him thump down a coin, and call for a bottle, then swung palely back to the slouched figure in the shadows. His boyish face was wooden but deep in his eyes lay something difficult to define, a guarded expression of strange, cold portent.

VII

Tom saw Elihu Gorman after 6:00 P.M. The banker's grip was weak, his palm clammy, when they shook. His face, too, seemed paler than it had the night before. Tom took a chair and sank down. He said: "Sorry I had to be late but word gets around in Beatty. I've had more cowmen wanting me to buy them out or back them, than you can shake a stick at." He studied Gorman; the wait had been hard on him, which is the way Tom had wanted it to be. "I'll tell you," he continued, cutting across the banker's opening words, "I've just about decided to hang and rattle a day or two over this. There might be other ways to invest that forty thousand."

"Yes, but. . . ."

"You see, I know the cattle business, Gorman, and I don't know this loaning business."

"But, Mister Barker, I told you . . . the loan will be guaranteed by the bank."

"I know," Tom said, getting to his feet. There was finality in his voice. "Just the same I'm going to hang and rattle until Monday or Tuesday. Thanks for your time and effort, Gorman."

Elihu did not arise from his desk. Tom let himself out of the bank and stood a moment on the plank walk, tasting the fullness of triumph. Northerly from the bank, in the smoky light of carriage lamps made fast to either side of the livery stable opening, three men were grouped in earnest conversation. He recognized one of them as Judge Montgomery. A second figure was the day hostler. The third man, with his back to Tom, was unrecognizable. He watched them a moment, then crossed to the hotel and went to his room.

Noise rose mutedly up from the roadway — the jingle of spurs, the stamp of boots and the hooting call of happy men. Tom blew down the lamp chimney, plunged his room into darkness, then stood by the window, looking down. Within a week Beatty would know whether he was top lash in the valley or a whipped cur riding out with his tail tucked under him. He smoked a cigarette. If he had to ride out, all right, but at least four men would not forget him as long as they lived: Judge Montgomery, Elihu Gorman, Moses Beach, and that old fogy, Sheriff Tim Pollard. He retired on that thought.

Sunday dawned with a blaze of saffron glory. Sunlight stole down the far hillsides, raced across the range, and burst upon Beatty with a soft brilliance that turned quickly to yellow, breathless heat. Tom awakened to the tolling of a church bell. He stared at the ceiling; he could close his eyes and hear that same bell tolling him out of bed as a boy. He and his mother had often gone to that church; since those days he had not once been inside a church. He swung out of bed, dressed, and went to the Queens & Aces Café for breakfast. There, unexpectedly, he met Tex and a high-breasted, long-legged girl, bold of eye and with a wide, full mouth that promised a generosity of spirit to match its size and heaviness. He nodded; the girl was from the Royal Antler; he'd often seen her there. But this meeting was different. In this setting she didn't look the same. No, he decided, it wasn't the setting, it was her attire. She had a subdued, well-cut dress with a primly high neckline; her hair was brushed severely back and in a bun at the nape of her neck. He squinted at Tex, at the buttoned suit coat, the peg-top pants, and yellow shoes — not boots. Tex's pale eyes avoided him and a slow stain mounted into his boyish face. *My God,* Tom thought, *they're going to church. Those two are going to church!*

"Yes, Mister Barker?"

"Coffee, fried meat, and potatoes."

He drummed on the counter, keeping cadence with the tolling bell. The girl threw him a wide smile. "I didn't know you ate, too," she said, laughing. "All I've ever seen you do is drink."

He continued to drum on the counter, gazing straight ahead at a garish curtain made hideous by enormous cabbage roses. From the corner of his eye he saw Tex nudge her and get uncomfortably to his feet. When they passed through the door, Tom twisted for another look. Miss Eloise — she had a way of walking. . . .

"Your coffee, Mister Barker."

He faced around and lifted the cup. When the cook returned with his platter of food, Tom said: "Mike, you go to the firemen's dances at the church house?"

"Yes, every year, Mister Barker. I wouldn't miss one."

"Why wouldn't you?"

"Everybody's there . . . all the pretty gals, the boys from the ranches, music, food. No, sir, I wouldn't miss one of them dances for the world."

Tom finished eating and left the café. He ran head-on into Judge Montgomery's daughter. If the choice had been his, he would have avoided the meeting; since he could not, he touched his hat and started past.

"Tom?"

It stopped him still. When they had been very young, she had called him that. He turned back, sweeping off his hat. "Yes'm."

"Are you going to church?"

"No'm."

Beneath her brows was the inquiring line of frank gray eyes. She had a beautiful, composed mouth; the lips lay together without pressure. He could see in them her flare of temper; she could charm a man or chill him to the marrow. She was slightly taller than the average woman, and maturity had given her a handsome figure, slightly full at breast and hip, and a face with both strong and pleasant contours. Her skin was creamy ordinarily, he could see, but now it was flushed by the steady-rising heat.

"Why not?"

A quick flash showed in his eyes, then died instantly; he forced a smile. "It's been so long I've forgotten how to act in a church, Toni."

Her smile came, long and soft. "Tom, you're the only one who ever called me Toni. Even yet . . . I'm Antoinette or Tonette. Except for Tim Pollard, of course."

He stood silently before her, courteous but impassive and distant. She regarded him levelly through an interval of silence. "Why . . . Tom?"

"Why . . . what?"

"Why did you come back?"

"You'll be late for prayer meeting, Toni."

Again the silence settled between them. She started to move, to turn away, then she called his name again, and he waited. "You'll be at the dance tonight?" she inquired.

"Yes'm. I reckon so."

"Should I save you a dance?"

Sweat broke out on his face and he could

feel the color mounting there in waves. He wanted to hasten away but instead he said gravely: "I'd like that, Toni."

She smiled then, and left him.

He thought of his room but restlessness drove him to the Royal Antler. Even with a bottle and glass and the morning hush of a saloon on Sunday, the restlessness did not leave. "Roy," he called to the bartender, who was the only other man in the room, "did you know Charley Ingersoll?"

"I knew him, Mister Barker."

"Do you know his brother?"

"Yes."

The barman leaned over the counter, looking round eyed at dark Tom Barker. In all these weeks this was the first time Tom had addressed him other than to call for a bottle. Also, Roy had heard the gossip and had as much curiosity as the next man, even though, in his trade, he had to work harder to conceal it than most men did.

"You've heard the talk . . . that he's going to hunt me up one of these days."

"I've heard it, Mister Barker."

Tom drained his glass before speaking again. "What's holding him back, Roy?"

"Nothin', I expect, Mister Barker. He'll come." Roy threw a long glance outward toward the shimmering road. "Clint's a freighter. He don't often get home."

"Well, I don't particularly want to kill him."

"I expect you're goin' to have to, though."

The bell ceased its tolling. Deep silence settled over the town. In the far distance a dog's barking rose keenly in the heat. Tom turned his back on the bar and gazed steadily out the window; beyond Beatty lay the pure flare of open range; beyond the range was a blue blur of rising hills, cowed now by midsummer's heat. Like all desert lands this was a country that went down deep into a man, remained there, a part of him, so long as he lived and breathed. It was for Tom Barker a solid part of memory, a segment of his life stream. He twisted, refilled his glass, and held it untouched in one fist, caught in the grip of memory.

He remembered her as a sweet child gripping the seat of a wagon watching him with solemn admiration. He recalled her, too, sitting beside him while a black Arizona night closed down around them, thick and mysterious, and only their tiny yellow-pointed campfire burning bravely while they pretended he was an Apache buck and she was his squaw. But his most vivid memory of her was the morning he went to her father full of a great and desperate fear, pleading for help. He could never forget how she had looked at him then, nor could he forget how her father had listened gravely, then had taken him to the sheriff to be rid of the squalor and sordidness he represented.

Four mounted men trotted into sight from the south, their horses pushing up gray gouts of dust as far as the Royal Antler hitch rail. There, the riders swung down, tied up, and started purposefully forward. Tom watched them briefly and put down his glass, arose, flung a coin upon the table, and walked out. He didn't want to hear laughter right then.

There has never been a man so wholly alone as the one who waits outside a church. Tom smoked a cigarette, leaning upon a store front with soft singing coming to him across the empty roadway. He thought of Moses Beach; how he was lying there, guarding Tom's secret unwillingly, and there was quite suddenly no flavor to the thought. But a hard man with a lifelong ambition to amount to something in the town that had turned him out could not easily change back to the boy he had once been. Willful energy lived in him; it showed in the uncompromising blackness of his eyes and in the set lines of his jaw and lips, and while, on the one hand he took no satisfaction from Beach's plight, on the other he could not, and would not, turn back.

The church was emptying. Women in bonnets and men in stiff collars and carefully greased shoes made their uncomfortable way through the heat. Judge Montgomery walked sedately beside Antoinette, and for just a moment black eyes and gray ones met in a distant clash and an electric shock traveled to Tom over the intervening distance. Then she was talking to a young man with glossy blond hair and did not again look in Tom's direction.

He threw down the cigarette and moved off toward the hotel. Behind him, coming out of the crowd, Tex and Miss Eloise paced evenly forward on the plank walk. They both saw his back moving away from them and each let a long glance linger on him. Miss Eloise said: "He's a strange person, isn't he?"

Tex was slow in replying. "He wasn't always that way, though, ma'am."

Liquid violet eyes lifted swiftly. "Oh? Do you know him?"

"Yes'm."

"But you didn't speak to him at the café."

"He wants it that way."

Miss Eloise's nose wrinkled. "You mean he doesn't want his friends to recognize him here in Beatty? Why, is he an outlaw?" Her eyes widened noticeably.

"No'm. That's just the way he wants it."

"Oh." Miss Eloise searched the empty plank walk for Tom Barker's figure but it had disappeared into the hotel. "Tex, will he be at the dance tonight?"

"I reckon he will. Leastwise he said he might show up."

"Well, would you care if I danced with him?"

Tex lowered his eyes to her face. "No'm, I wouldn't care. Only I'll give you odds he won't ask you to dance."

Miss Eloise's round eyes were momentarily lost behind a slow, feline blink. "What kind of odds, honey?" she asked silkily.

Tex looked rueful. He said: "I just remembered something. I ain't going to bet with you."

"*Aren't* going to bet with me."

"All right . . . aren't. It's the same thing anyway."

"Tex . . . ?"

"Yes'm."

"Why's everyone scairt of him? Is he truly a gunman?"

"He ain't no gunman, and if anyone's scairt of him, I expect they got a reason to be. He was born and partly raised-up in this town."

"I didn't know that."

"Well, he was. And he's got a grudge against it, too."

"Against the town? You mean against the whole town?"

"Yes'm."

"I declare, I never heard of such a thing before."

Tex turned thoughtful. "Listen to me," he said quickly. "Don't you breathe a word of what I've told you to a living soul. You understand?"

"Don't worry, I won't. Cross my heart."

Tex's boyish face resumed its normal open expression. "Shall I meet you at the dance or fetch you from the Royal Antler?"

"From the Royal Antler, silly. I'm not going to pay my own way into that dance."

Tex smiled, then he laughed. "That'd be something, wouldn't it . . . you paying your own way to a dance?"

VIII

When darkness came down, the mystery of the night closed in. Tom was still in his room when he heard the musicians start playing. He examined himself in the mirror as best he could — it was not a very large piece of glass — then crossed to the window and stood a moment, watching couples strolling toward the plank pavilion beside the church. There was an elusive feeling of excitement in him that would not be pinned down, hard as he tried to catch it in words. He saw Tex enter the Royal Antler and reappear shortly with Miss Eloise on his arm. He smiled flintily; if Tex wasn't careful, he was going to find himself with a ring in his nose. Well, no matter how good a cowboy a man was, he would not be young forever, and in the end perhaps it was better to have a woman and children and a piece of land, a place to rest your head when the storms came. He shrugged and started for the door. It would not be hard to tame Tex Earle; he'd always had the seeds of domesticity in him anyway.

It was a fluid crowd that eddied around him as he approached the pavilion. The music was loud and lively. Laden tables groaned under the weight of food and four huge punch bowls stood brimming. A dozen young men were clustered around one particular bowl and their mischievous grins told the story of a smuggled bottle that had been emptied into the punch there. He caught a glimpse of Antoinette whirling past on her father's arm, and he thought, in that brief moment, that her searching gaze had come to rest with something like relief when she saw him. Tex and Miss Eloise pranced by and Roy the bartender, hair neatly plastered, face set woodenly to endure discomfort, glided past. Even Elihu Gorman was dancing, a sturdy woman near his own age in his arms.

When a quiet voice drawled at his side, he turned to see Sheriff Pollard slouching there, fierce mustache waxed and set, faded eyes crinkled in a tolerant smile. "You got a gun under that coat, Mister Barker?"

"Yes. Is it against the law to have one here?"

"Nope."

"Then why did you ask?"

"Because Clint Ingersoll's wagons were seen southeast of town this afternoon." Pollard continued to regard the dancers. "He'll likely show up here tonight."

Tom was jostled from behind; he moved closer to the sheriff to permit several laughing couples to squeeze past. "I can't stop him from coming here," he said.

"No," Pollard conceded, "you can't. Would you . . . if you could?"

"Yes."

"Why? You worried?"

"No."

"Mebbe you should be. They say Clint's fair to middlin' fast with a handgun."

"That's not fast enough," Tom replied, and edged away through the crowd.

Sheriff Pollard watched the broad retreating back, and, when Jack Havestraw came up, he turned and said: "Y'know, it's hard to like a man that don't like you . . . but it isn't always hard to respect 'em."

The youthful deputy looked around at the crowd. "Who?" he asked, not seeing Tom.

"Barker. I was just talkin' to him. I don't think he wants to use that gun so bad, after all."

"Oh. Did you get the answers back on him yet?"

"Nope. And likely when I do, I'll already know all I want to know about him. I got a feelin' about that."

The sheriff moved off in the same direction Tom had taken. People called his name, jostled him, and offered him drinks. It made him feel good, as a lawman, to be liked rather than disliked. Once, he caught a fleeting glimpse of Tom Barker talking to a high-breasted girl. It was Miss Eloise and the flashing smile she wore suggested that perhaps it wasn't altogether a coincidence that, at that precise moment, the dance caller held up his fiddle for the crowd's attention and bellowed: "Ladies' choice, gents. Ladies' choice."

There was more than challenge in the violet eyes in front of Tom Barker; there was interest and curiosity, and perhaps flirtation as well. He took her arm and went forward; the music commenced, louder and wilder it seemed to him, and they whirled away. He had not danced in years and her closeness troubled him. He felt the rhythm of her body and was conscious of the clean smell of her hair. She held her dazzling smile and gazed directly into his eyes.

"You are a good dancer, Mister Barker," Eloise said, then, before he spoke, she rushed on: "Can I call you Tom?"

His discomfort increased: "Yes'm, you can."

"And you call me Eloise."

He inclined his head slightly. She was dancing very close to him and he could feel the ripple of flesh and muscle. He also knew many eyes watched them and winced from the thought of Antoinette.

The dance finally ended. Tom escorted Miss Eloise to the sidelines and made a quick exit. He did not see Tex push through and claim Eloise for the next dance, and so he missed the pale light in Earle's eyes that crystallized into hardness as Eloise talked.

Tom was nearing the outer fringe of people when a chirping voice hailed him. "Nice dance, ain't it, Mister Barker?" He looked around and down. It was Mike from the Queens & Aces. He nodded, and pushed past.

There was a scent of dust in the air and shadows twisted and turned where the lanterns hung. On the side wall of the church gigantic figures jerked and plunged, their shadowy distortions trailing off into deep murk. A restless bubble of talk quivered on the air; people continued to arrive; laughter, flashing eyes, and flushed faces moved forward in a strong blur.

"Tom?"

He was making a cigarette. His hands grew still as he twisted. She was smiling up at him, but there was something in her gray eyes that only partly smiled.

"You dance very well."

He finished the cigarette, lit it, and blew out a gust of smoke. "So do you," he said.

She came closer and leaned upon a bone-gray old cottonwood log that had long ago been shored up as a bench. "Do you recognize very many of them?" she asked.

He shook his head, watching people pass. "No, not very many, Toni. Only a very few.

I guess twelve years is a long time on the frontier."

"It is. It's a long time anywhere."

"Would you care to dance?"

"If you want to."

He looked at her. "But you'd rather not."

"I'd rather walk," she replied.

They inched their way clear of the throng and she took his arm. He was aware of her nearness, of the swaying of their bodies along the plank walk through the deserted town.

"Do you remember the time you made me climb into the church bell tower with you?"

"Yes, I remember. You were scairt to death."

She smiled, keeping step with him. "And the night we both got tanned because we were an Apache warrior and his squaw and stayed out after sundown?"

He smiled.

"Why, Tom?"

He made no immediate reply, but he knew what she meant. It took a moment to bring himself back from the past, though, and with the rush through time came also his defenses.

They continued to walk along, neither breaking the silence until finally he said:

"For a lot of reasons, Toni."

"Wise reasons?"

He sought for words and failed to find the right ones, and through his thoughts her words came again.

"Revenge? To show Beatty you are as good as it is?"

He stopped and swung her around. "I wouldn't have to be very good for that, Toni." His gaze was brittle. "To show Beatty I'm better than it is."

"Then," she said gravely, "you shouldn't have come back, Tom."

He dropped his arms. The quarter moon lay its soft silver light across her face. He saw its stillness, its beauty and strength. He also saw the deep and unknown things in her eyes and averted his face. She took his arm and gently propelled him forward again.

"I think there is something in this world that can destroy men more surely than bullets, Tom. Hate. It would break my heart if that happened to you. When we were children, you were my ideal, my hero." She paused; then: "But there's not much left in you from those days."

"How do you know?"

"Do you remember what Abraham Lincoln said about men's faces?"

"No."

"He said that every man is responsible for what shows in his face after he is thirty."

"And what you see in mine you don't like."

"I didn't say that, Tom. It isn't so easy to destroy your gods. What I said was . . . hate can ruin you."

"I don't hate, Toni. I don't hate Beatty or the men here who. . . ."

"Are you sure of that, Tom?"

"I'm sure."

"Then what is it you feel toward them?"

"Contempt, I guess."

"But they're good men, Tom. Listen to me, I've known them all much longer than you have."

"But you were not the son of a drunk freighter or a woman who ran off with another man. You were Judge Montgomery's kid, Toni."

"Let me finish," she said. "I've known them longer than you have. They are human, Tom. They make mistakes. Their judgments are not always good. But they are as good and honest as any men are, anywhere, and it's wrong for you to scorn them for their errors." Her grip on his arm tightened. "How can you sit in judgment on them, Tom?"

"Why shouldn't I?"

Her step slowed, then halted altogether. She looked up at him, searched his eyes and his features, then she looked away and they continued to walk.

She said, in a thoroughly impersonal manner: "You've changed more than I'd guessed, Tom." She said it as though it were a contingency that no longer mattered; there was a dullness in her voice and her hand fell away from his arm.

He walked along with angry, troubled thoughts. They had been very close once, but that was long ago. It was far away; it was in another life; he had long since become hard and dedicated and he could not possibly change after one stroll in the moonlight.

"I should have known, when you killed Charley Ingersoll." His lips drew out in a flat line. He might have spoken but her words cut across his marshaling thoughts. "I should have seen then that you do sit in judgment over people. Only I didn't think of that, then. I only thought . . . Tom is back. Life will be like it was."

"Toni, they sat in judgment on me, or have you forgotten that?"

"And so," she intoned in the same lifeless voice, "that gives you the right to sit in judgment on them." She looked at the buildings around them and slowed to a halt. "Let's go back, Tom."

The walk back was made mostly in silence and none of the earlier buoyancy remained in their steps. Neither of them was aware of the blond man following them through the soft summer night, his face tense and angry, his light eyes fixed with strong hatred upon Tom's broad back.

People began to pass them; a few were elderly couples but more were young girls leaning on the arms of happy youths. There was a sprinkling of lean cowboys from the ranches walking proudly beside town girls. Near the stone water trough Tom took Toni's arm and steered her into the bland darkness of an ancient cottonwood tree. Strains of music carried easily this far and overhead, through a filigree of dusty leaves, the high, brilliant stars and the capsized moon rode serenely in a cobalt heaven.

"You'd ask me to give up all the plans I've made for the last twelve years, wouldn't you, Toni?"

She shook her head slightly, slowly. "No, Tom, I wouldn't ask you to give up anything. That isn't something others can ask of you. It's something you've got to ask of yourself."

He made a cigarette. She heard the full sweep of breath in his chest. He moved a short distance off and sank down on the lip of the old water trough. He sat with cigarette smoke eddying up around his face, with his elbows on his knees, and with his lips set in a hard, tough line.

She turned her head, gazing at him. Each curve of his body registered in her mind. She looked for, but did not find, the boy she had once known. Now, in his place, she saw only the signs of a strong man's reticence, his certain confidence, his tempered hardness, and the full sweep of his passion, which would be as hot as fire in anger — or in love.

"I think we'd better go back," she said. "Dad will be wondering about me."

He got off the stonework but went forward only as far as the tree, where she was leaning. He seemed to want to say something, but the held-back expression in his face told her, whatever it was, he would not say it. The stillness went on like that, full of unexpressed and puzzling emotions. Then he groped for her hand and held it tightly in his grip, too lost within the tiny sphere of his own absorption to notice a vague shadow fade into a doorway, watching them, nor see another shadow stop suddenly over by the

Royal Antler, then slide forward, moving in behind the first shadow.

He released her hand and she pushed forward off the tree. Suddenly, looking up, she saw only the moving blur of his face, the full sweep of his shoulders against the night. He looked very sad and very solemn, and his dark eyes were blacker than a well's depths. Both his hands came up, dropped upon her shoulders, and pulled her in. Her head was tilted; one hand came up to rest against his chest with gentleness, and he kissed her with soft, long pressure, with a painful hunger that seared into her mind. When he released her, she clung to his arm for a moment, then without a word they started forward out of the semidarkness, pacing slowly together back toward the sound of music.

"Toni?"

"Yes."

"Should I apologize?"

"No, Tom."

They were on the fringe of the crowd now; people nodded and smiled and shouldered them this way and that way. He touched her, stopping, wide-legged, bracing into the stream of humanity, seeing nothing but the directness of her gaze.

"When we were kids . . . ," he began.

"That's gone now," she said swiftly. "That's all over, Tom. It might never have been at all." She freed her arm and cast him a final look. "That's what the kiss was for. Memories, Tom. It was a salute to something that was very sweet, very innocent, and wonderful. Good night, Tom."

IX

He walked through the crowd, low in spirit, and did not at once hear the voice at his side.

"Tom . . . you said it would be all right for me to call you that."

He looked into Eloise's violet eyes and made a mechanical smile.

"Folks are still dancing, Tom."

He stopped, looking over her head. "Where's Tex?"

"He went to the saloon for a minute. He'll be coming up soon. About that dance. . . ."

He didn't feel like dancing, but he took her arm and pushed forward, and they danced. Once, near the pavilion's edge, he glimpsed Judge Montgomery in heated conversation with two men, then other dancing couples cut across the line of vision and he lost them. Finally the musicians ended their sweaty labors with a crashing finale and Tom led Miss Eloise to the sidelines and left her.

The crowd was not quite as thick as before. Now, there was standing and sitting room. There was also a noisy drunk being forcibly escorted away from the area by Tim Pollard on one side and young Jack Havestraw on the other side. Men smiled broadly and their girls giggled.

"Enjoying yourself, Mister Barker?"

It was Judge Montgomery, and, although his words had been affable enough, there was a hot, wrathful glitter to his eyes.

Tom nodded, waiting.

"Can I have a few words with you?"

"Certainly."

They walked beyond the milling crowd and Judge Montgomery turned finally, lamplight showing his face to be pale and agitated.

"I understand you are in the hay and grain business," he said, faint acid in his tone.

Tom felt for his tobacco sack and began manufacturing a cigarette. "I am."

"I also understand that you bribed my former night man at the barn to tell you how soon I'd be needing feed."

Tom kept his eyes on the cigarette. Part of his bribe had been for keeping this information from the judge. He felt both mean and outraged, and he made no reply at all.

"I can guess your purpose, Mister Barker."

"Can you, Judge?"

"Quite easily, in fact."

Tom lit the cigarette and looked steadily into the older man's face over its burning tip. "Did you bring me out here to call me names, Judge?"

Montgomery's jowls rippled, his eyes burned with a fierce light, but he controlled his voice. "No, Mister Barker. I asked you out here to sell me some hay and grain."

"How much do you want?"

"Twenty tons of hay and ten tons of grain. What is your price?"

"Eleven dollars for the hay and. . . ."

"Eleven dollars! Hell! I've never paid more than three dollars a ton in my life!"

"Judge, you asked my price and I told you. You don't have to buy from me."

"Barker, this is robbery," choked Montgomery. "Highway robbery. You'll not get away with it! I know what you've done . . . taking options."

Tom shrugged. "Ride it out," he said evenly. "If you know about the options, you also know they're only for sixty days. Just ride it out for sixty days, Judge, and maybe you'll get the hay for three dollars again."

Tom exhaled slowly. "And again . . . maybe you won't, too. I may exercise those options."

"You won't and you know it, Barker."

"I don't know it," Tom replied. "I'm arranging right now to haul that hay to San Carlos. If Uncle Sam takes it, Judge, he'll take every blade of it."

Judge Montgomery was breathing heavily. He plunged fisted hands into his trouser pockets and said: "I could have hay hauled in."

Tom's eyes lit up with cold humor. "I looked into that before I took those options, Judge. It'd cost fifteen dollars a ton to load your loft through freighters. My price is only eleven a ton."

"Barker. . . ."

"Listen, Judge, you're out of hay and grain. You can't operate a livery barn without them. Your profits are good. You make more money from that barn than you do on the bench. Eleven dollars a ton isn't going to put you out of business. I think you'd better pay it."

"I'll see you in hell first!"

Tom turned on his heel and walked back toward the pavilion.

Judge Montgomery remained stiff and outraged on the far fringe of the crowd. He had never been a profane man or he would have sworn savagely at that precise moment.

Tom came upon the sheriff, mopping his face with a large blue bandanna. He smiled at him. "Hot night for escorting rambunctious drunks," he allowed. Pollard stuffed the bandanna in a hip pocket and nodded.

"Hot for other things, too," he said. "I just heard about your hay deals." He squinted at Tom and wagged his head. "You know, if you was working steady at making enemies in Beatty, you couldn't do it no better'n you are now. I worry about you, boy."

"You don't have to, Sheriff. As for the hay deals . . . isn't that how businessmen get ahead?"

Pollard's squint remained. "It's legal, if that's what you're drivin' at, but it's sure gettin' folks down on you."

"Are they down on Beach and Gorman and the judge? Are they down on you, Sheriff, for doing what you have to do to make a living?"

Pollard rolled his eyes. "Why is it," he cried, "that sharpers always got logic on their side when they're cornered?"

"I'm not cornered, Sheriff. Far from it. I've got money to invest and I aim to make money with it." Tom dropped the cigarette and ground it underfoot. "If you think I'm cornered, you see where I am in another month."

He was moving away, toward the roadway, when Sheriff Pollard said: "Dead. That's what you'll be in another month, Barker. Dead and buried."

Tom continued on his way. He walked south nearly as far as the stone water trough, then angled through the dusty roadway toward the hotel. The far side of the road was drowned in shadows and darkness; he did not discern slow movement along a northerly store front, but behind him, rigid beside the old cottonwood tree, another detached figure caught the gliding outline and shifted to face it.

"You, there! Barker!"

It was a soft, sharp call. It rode down the night to Tom with unmistakable meaning. He stopped still, then began to turn very slowly. The silhouette back by the cottonwood tree moved swiftly northward until lost in the night, then cut rapidly across to Tom's side of the roadway and came down behind the emerging blond man who was walking flat-footedly toward Tom, right arm bent slightly and fingers crabbed.

"You see me now, Barker?"

Tom turned a little more, brushing back the right side of his coat as he did so. "I see you," he said, finding much in the other man's outline to remind him of dead Charley Ingersoll.

"I never yet shot a man in the back, Barker, but I could've blown you in two a dozen times tonight."

Tom waited for the man to step off the plank walk into the dust; when he finally did, still walking purposefully forward, the same kind of blond hair was visible, the same flat features and brutish expression that Charley Ingersoll had had.

"You know who I am, Barker?"

"I can guess."

"Let's hear your guess."

"You're Clint Ingersoll."

The blond man halted fifty feet away and tilted back his head. Moonlight softened the harshness of his face and hid his eyes in sunken shadows. "You're dead right. I'm Clint Ingersoll. Did you figure I'd be scared to face you?"

"No," Tom replied levelly, catching a flicker of movement twenty feet behind Ingersoll, along the front of the Queens & Aces Café, and incorrectly thinking it was either Tim Pollard or some confederate of Ingersoll's.

"But you sweated a little, waitin', didn't you?"

Tom said no again, in the same quiet way, and added: "I was hopin' you wouldn't think you had to do this."

"You was hopin' I'd forget you murdered my brother?"

"I didn't murder him. He drew on me. What did you expect me to do . . . stand there and get shot?"

"That's what's goin' to happen to you now, Barker. You're goin' to stand there an' get shot."

Tom saw the distant shadow behind Ingersoll move out clearly and straighten up out of a crouch. He saw the cocked gun lift to bear and heard a voice he recognized say: "Ingersoll, you make a move toward that gun and you'll be dead before you get it out."

The blond man turned to stone. Not a face muscle moved. Then, very slowly, his lips curled in a twist of contempt and he said: "If you wasn't scared, Barker, why'd you hire a bodyguard?"

Tom moved forward into the road. He watched Tex ease Ingersoll's gun out and throw it down. "I have no bodyguard, Ingersoll. He happens to be a friend of mine."

Tex spoke from behind the disarmed freighter. "He's been shagging you all night, Tom. I've been watching him."

"Good thing for him you was," Ingersoll growled.

Tex's hard laughter was short. "You damned muleskinner, Tom Barker'd kill you with his left hand. You'll maybe never know it, feller, but I saved your bacon tonight."

"Give me back my gun and let's see about that!"

Tex swore and started to push the gun forward. Tom stopped him with a word, then he went still closer and gazed into Clint Ingersoll's face. There was hate and unreasoning fury there. Tom sighed, bobbed his head toward a dogtrot between two buildings, and started forward. Tex prodded his prisoner along. They emerged into a back lot where broken pottery lay like bones in the moonlight. Tom removed his coat and gun belt and faced Ingersoll. He was standing relaxed and resigned and was unprepared when Ingersoll dug his heels into the ground and hurled himself forward, driving Tom back, low and hard, until his shoulders struck wood and his ears rang from impact. He was wise enough, however, to lie limply in the freighter's grip until he had one arm free, then he sledged downward with the full power of his arm and Ingersoll's knees sprung inward and his grip softened.

Tom spun sideways and got free. Ingersoll

was shaking his head. A sullen purple bruise was fleshing up behind his ear. He cursed and rushed forward a second time, head low, arms extended. Tom moved forward instead of backward and threw a crashing fist that made Ingersoll stumble. Before the blond man could recover he had him by the shoulders, slammed him against a building, and, when Ingersoll bounced off, he swung his body weight in behind his right fist and buried a granite-hard set of knuckles in Ingersoll's belly. The freighter's breath whooshed out and his mouth hung far open. Tom hit him again, and again, then he stepped back and Ingersoll slumped at the shoulders, bent in the middle, broke over at the knees, and went down into the refuse to lie crumpled and without movement.

Tom moved away, toward his coat and shell belt. He was sucking hot night air into the bottoms of his lungs when Tex moved quickly forward to hold his coat.

"He looked tougher'n that," Tex said, helping Tom shrug into the coat. "Hell, I think I could've taken him, myself."

Tom grinned, breathing deeply. "There he is, if you want to try."

Tex bent a long look on the unconscious man. "Why didn't you just kill him?" he asked.

"You sure got a short memory," Tom said, drawing upright again, shifting his holstered gun to its normal position. "There you sat, up there by that damned creek, preaching me a sermon about being a potential gunman. . . ."

"This was different," Tex protested. "He was all set to draw on you."

"Well, why didn't you let him, then?"

Tex rubbed his jaw and scowled perplexedly. "Damned if I know," he said. Then his face brightened. "Wait, I'll get some water and douse him. When he comes around. . ."

"Go bed down," Tom said dryly. "I don't want to shoot the simpleton any more'n I wanted to dance with Miss Eloise."

Tex's shoulders pulled up straight. He faced Tom.

"An' that's another thing," he said heatedly. "She told. . . ."

"Tex, do me a favor, will you? Marry her or whatever you got in mind. Right now I'm tired. I don't want to fight with anybody." Tom cocked his head. "We've run together a long time, haven't we?"

"Yes."

"Did you ever see me try to cut in on another man's woman?"

"No, I guess not."

"Then for gosh sakes go bed down, will you, and just remember one thing. I'll be waiting for you up by the creek tomorrow."

Tex prodded Ingersoll with his toe. "What about him? Tom, maybe you don't want no war, but he does. After this licking he'll want one worse than ever."

Tom considered Clint Ingersoll's inert figure. Tex was probably right; they would meet again. Maybe not. You could never tell about other people. He shrugged. "If he comes around again, I guess next time I'll kill him, Tex."

They parted then, Tex heading for the livery stable loft and Tom bound for his hotel room.

X

He and Tex relaxed in the shade along the creek on Monday. These weekly rendezvous were the bright spot in his life now. Here, he could fully relax. This morning, the out-of-character sensitivity he'd sensed in Tex lately was entirely gone, too, and that cheered him a little. He gazed at his friend of many campfires and spoke in a voice as dry as wind rattling cornhusks.

"It wasn't altogether Miss Eloise, was it?"

"What d'you mean, Tom?"

"Cut it out," Tom said shortly. "Fool anyone under the sun . . . but me. I've known you too long."

Tex was smoothing the dust in front of him with a stick. "No," he admitted. "It wasn't just Eloise. I expect it wasn't Eloise at all, Tom." He etched a Texas brand into the smoothed dirt with methodical detail. "I was getting kind of sick of this thing, to tell you the truth." He threw the stick aside. "Y'know, when that ugly little storekeeper got took down sick, I got to remembering something an old Indian once told me. If you think evil about someone, they get sick. That ain't my way of fighting, Tom. If I got a grudge, why I take up my gun and go out 'n' settle it. What you've been doing sort of . . . well, it sort of makes me ashamed. It don't seem manly, somehow."

Tom tugged his hat forward to shade his eyes. "Listen, Tex, you can't call out a judge or a storekeeper or a sheriff. They won't fight you. So, you meet them on their own ground. That's the only way you can beat them. That's all I'm trying to do."

"I reckon," Tex said resignedly. He let off a big sigh. "But I still think it's better to come right out in the open when you got fight talk to make."

"I did that last night with Ingersoll."

"I know, Tom. I thought about that last night in bed. But this other stuff, well, if that's the way it's got to be, all right, go ahead. I'll string along, but it's not my way at all."

Tom smoked a cigarette. They sat in silence for a while, then Tom said: "I'm in a helluva fix. I broke Beach and I've got the only man in town who can bail him out eating out of my hand."

"Who's that?"

"The banker."

"What's the fix, then?"

"The judge."

"Hell, Tom, you got the hay an' he's hurtin' for some. You got him, too."

Tom continued to gaze at nothing. "You don't understand. It's his daughter. . . ."

"I understand all right," Tex said carelessly. "I saw you kiss her under the cottonwood, Tom." Tex twisted on the ground. "I don't approve of hitting a man through his girl . . . but like I said, I'll string along. For a little while longer anyway."

"I wasn't hitting at Judge Montgomery through Toni."

Tex looked disbelieving. "No? Then what were you doing?"

Tom pushed his legs out, crossed them at the ankles, and stared at his toes. "I . . . I'm not sure what I was doing. But I don't want to do it again, I can tell you that."

Tex picked up a blade of grass and began chewing it. He stared steadily at Tom and several minutes later he threw back his head and roared with laughter.

Tom straightened up. "What's so damned funny?"

"Nothing," Tex said, choking on his mirth. "I just felt like baying at the moon."

"Well, don't do it so loudly, you idiot. Someone'll hear and come looking."

Tex subsided. He chewed a while longer on the grass, then he moved as though to arise. "Tom, I ain't smart like you. I never was. I recognized that six, eight years back. But there's sure Lord some things I can see that you sure as hell can't see. I can tell you that for gospel truth."

"What can't I see?"

Tex stood up and dusted his trousers off. "Never mind," he said. "The sky'll fall on you one of these days . . . then you'll see." He squinted at the sun. "About time to be getting back. Finnerty wants me to make the drive to San Carlos with him. What about it?"

"It won't take more'n two weeks, will it?"

"Less than that, Tom."

"Then go ahead. I won't need you for a

while anyway."

"Couple more things."

"Shoot."

"You ain't aiming to humble that old sheriff, are you?"

"Yes."

"Dammit, Tom, he's an old man."

"He owes me something, Tex."

Earle's pale eyes clouded over, but he said no more on the subject of Tim Pollard. Instead, he spat out the grass and said: "How long you think you can go on bluffing on a busted flush? I know how much money you've spent lately . . . on all that there hay and what-not. You ain't got but a couple hundred dollars left, Tom."

"I know that and you know it," Tom conceded. "But no one else does." He arose and stretched. "Now comes the big one, Tex."

"What do you mean?"

"When you get back from San Carlos, you'll find out. I'll either be spoon-feeding that damned town and its crop of righteous fat-backs, or I'll be saddling up to ride on. One or the other."

"I got my ideas about which," Tex opined, and went to his horse, caught up the reins, and mounted. "Just wait for me to get back is all. I'd sort of like to be in on the finish of this thing, since I got roped in on the beginning."

"I'll wait. And, Tex . . . while you're at San Carlos, find out what the Army's paying for hay, will you?"

"Sure. *Adiós,* Tom."

"Adiós."

He rode back the usual way, entering Beatty from the south, and the first person he saw was Tim Pollard's young deputy. Havestraw threw him a reserved nod and called out: "Elihu Gorman's looking for you!"

Tom said — "Thanks." — and dismounted at the livery stable. The hostler who faced him was a new man, nearly as large as Tom was, and disagreeable-looking. "You Mister Barker?" he asked, studying Tom's features as though to identify them from a description. Tom nodded, holding out the reins. "You ain't welcome here," the hostler said, pocketing his hands and leaving Tom standing there with the reins outstretched. "Boss's orders."

Tom continued to regard the man through a moment of blossoming antagonism, then he turned abruptly and crossed to the hotel hitch rail. As he was mounting the stairs to his room, he spoke over his shoulder to the clerk. "Have someone find a place for my horse. Not the livery barn. Understand?"

"Yes, Mister Barker."

Tom was unlocking his door when a man's deep voice greeted him from behind. He turned. Elihu Gorman was arising from a ladder-back chair. Tom pushed open the door and motioned for the banker to precede him inside. The encounter at the livery barn had left him feeling angry. He closed the door, watched the way Gorman folded over onto a chair, and flung his hat on the dresser.

"I have all the data on that loan for you," the banker said with false briskness.

"I told you, I'd think about it."

Tom crossed to the window and began making a cigarette. Gorman watched his every move with anxious eyes. "This thing can't wait," he said. "It's the best investment in the area. Someone else will come along."

"Let them," Tom said, lighting up. He shot a slow glance at Gorman's face, noted its paleness, its poorly concealed agitation. He had been keeping track of the weeks; Beach and Gorman didn't have much time left.

Gorman was starting to speak again when a quick rap echoed from the door. Tom called out: "Who is it?"

"The desk clerk, Mister Barker. Doctor

Spence is downstairs looking for Mister Gorman."

Gorman looked annoyed but he arose. "Mister Barker . . .?"

"I'll give you a definite answer by the end of the week," Tom said. "And meanwhile, to start our association off, I want to see how good your bank's judgment is."

"Sir? I don't exactly follow you?"

Tom removed his wallet, extracted a thick sheaf of papers, and held them out. "Take them," he growled, and, when Gorman extended his hand, Tom said: "Arrange a five-thousand-dollar loan on those options for me. Put the money in an account for me. I won't be needing it, but it'll establish our relationship."

Gorman was gazing at the papers. "Hay and grain options?" he said, his voice rising.

"That's right," Tom answered, crossing to the door and holding it open. "I'll be over to see you within the next few days."

After Gorman left, Tom stood thoughtfully frowning for a moment, then scooped up his hat, and left the hotel with long strides.

It was mid-afternoon. Except for the coolness of the Royal Antler and one or two other such places in Beatty, there was little relief to be found from the punishing heat.

Tom took his usual table at the Royal Antler and nodded silently as Roy brought forth a bottle and glass.

"Seen you at the dance," Roy said quietly, letting his eyes cut quickly across Barker's dark and brooding face. "Seen you later, too."

Something about the way Roy said "later" made Tom look up.

"Behind the café, I mean. You and your friend and Clint Ingersoll."

Tom poured a drink, offered the glass to Roy who declined, and tossed the liquor off neat. "You've got pretty good eyesight," said Tom in a tone as quiet as the one the bartender had used. "Where were you?"

"In the outhouse behind the saloon here." Roy straightened up. "That was quite a battle, Mister Barker. Wish I'd seen the start of it, though."

"That was the start of it."

Roy shook his head. "I mean when you two first met. Y'see, I know Clint pretty well. He'd use his gun before he'd use his fists. I'd have liked to have seen you disarm him."

"It wasn't me who did that, Roy."

"Oh? Tex, then. Well, you two're quite a pair, Mister Barker."

"Are we?"

"Yep." Roy lowered his voice. "A feller in my job's got nothin' much to do during slack times but watch people."

"Meaning?"

"Hell's bells, Mister Barker. I spotted you and Tex tradin' looks three weeks back."

Tom poured a second drink but did not lift the glass. "You told anyone else about this, Roy?" he asked.

"Naw. Ain't any of my business, really."

Tom continued to regard the glass of whiskey. Roy probably had not told anyone else; barmen were notoriously close-mouthed. Still, what one man had noticed, others might also have noticed. He suddenly felt no desire for more liquor.

"Maybe we'd ought to keep it like that," he said, arising.

Roy smiled. He raised one hand and touched the graying hair over his ear.

"See that there gray," he said. "A man in my job don't live that long unless he learns damned early to button his lip."

Tom nodded and started to move past.

"Mister Barker?"

"Yeah?"

"Clint's still around."

"Making fight talk is he, Roy?"

"Not that I know of, but just the same you'll want to grow an eye in the back of your head."

Tom gazed steadily at the bartender. "He didn't strike me as a bushwhacker, Roy."

The barman shrugged. "Who knows what a man'll do? You beat him fair with your hands, Mister Barker, and he's heard the talk by now of how you handle a gun. Them things're usually enough to make a man do a little figurin' . . . if he's plumb set on killin' somebody."

Tom fished a $20 gold piece out of his pocket and put it in the bartender's hand. "Thanks, I'll take your advice," he said, moving off toward the door.

Outside, the plank walk was nearly deserted and heat waves arose in dancing ranks from the roadway. Tom was walking north, past a bench in front of Beach's store, when Sheriff Tim Pollard came through the doorway and met him.

Tom nodded. The sheriff's eyes pinched down suddenly and he caught Tom's arm. "Set on the bench with me a minute," he said. "I know somethin' that might interest you."

Tom sat. Pollard fished for his pocket knife, opened it, and began leisurely to pare his fingernails. "You seen Doc Spence today?" he asked.

"No."

"Seen Gorman, the banker?"

"A couple of hours ago. Why, what of it?"

"Well, a real strange thing happened this mornin'. Doc Spence calls it a medical miracle."

"Then it surely must be," Tom said dryly.

The sheriff chuckled. "I take it you don't much cotton to Doc Spence."

Tom put both hands palms down on the bench. "Is that what you stopped me for . . . to talk about Spence?"

"No. Everything in good time, boy. Just relax."

Tom's glance sharpened. The old devil knew something; there was no mistaking that look on his face. Tom settled back and stifled an impatient curse.

Pollard clicked the knife closed and turned to gaze at Tom. "Moses Beach got his voice back this morning."

XI

In the stifling silence of his room Tom sprawled on the bed thinking. Moses Beach knew, somehow, that he had given Finnerty the money to redeem his note at the bank. The proof that he knew was in the way he had sent immediately for Elihu Gorman when he could talk. To warn Gorman about him. What would Gorman's reaction be? He would of course refuse to loan money on the options, for one thing, and he might even suspect that Tom had met Evan Houston and had learned from the cowman that Gorman had offered Houston Finnerty's ranch before the bank had been in a position to foreclose. He gazed fixedly at the ceiling. Well, let Gorman think what he wished; it did not change anything. Gorman and Beach still had less than ten days to repay their loan and the thirty percent interest. Tom's lips curled. Beach would have another stroke. He smiled more broadly and leaped up, went to the window, and gazed down at the road.

The shadows were moving in. There was a faint and acrid breeze blowing in from the range. Far out the hills squatted in faded patience awaiting dusk, and surcease from the blinding sun rays and moonlight. Somewhere, beyond town, a bull roared and mules whinnied. There was a freight outfit camped there somewhere. He thought immediately of Clint Ingersoll. What a fool he'd been; he should have killed him. Why hadn't he?

He crossed to the washstand, mopped at his face, combed his hair, and hunched into his coat. He hadn't, he told himself, because of Tex. He hadn't wanted to lose the respect he'd kept these past years. No, that wasn't altogether the reason, either. Antoinette Montgomery was mixed up in it some way. Kissing her under the cottonwood tree had done something to him that night, had somehow softened the resolve in him.

He moved to the door, opened it, and passed through. Tex had been only partly right when he had told Ingersoll he had saved his bacon. Toni had been responsible, also, for Ingersoll's remaining alive.

The lobby was empty when he passed through and halted briefly in the swift-falling dusk beyond. Summer night air was good, he thought, drawing his lungs full of it. He was moving, turning south on the plank walk, when the shot came. He heard it clearly for the fleetingest part of a second before the hammer blow knocked him forward to his knees, pushing his breath out in a loud grunt. His mind said to go flat and roll, to get away from there. He went fully down and scrabbled through the roadway's dust, automatically drawing and cocking his gun as he did so.

There was no immediate sense of pain, only breathlessness. It was not a new sensation; he'd had it once before, when he'd fought a wild Mexican in Wichita. The result of that battle still bothered him occasionally, a sliver of deeply embedded lead in his right hip. There was a frothy mist forming before him. He strained to see through it. It widened, deepened, turned crimson. He shook his head irritably, struggling to find the peril lying beyond. Dimly men's voices came, raised in excitement. His head began to roll forward. He fought to hold it up; it went slowly downward despite his heroic efforts; then a wonderful feeling of pleasant drowsiness came.

"It's Barker, Sheriff. He's shot, by God."

Pollard came up and stopped, looking down. "Uhn-huh," he conceded. "Damned if he isn't. Jack, fetch Doc Spence. Couple you other boys give me a hand packin' him to his room upstairs."

"Nasty-lookin' wound," someone said, with much more interest than sympathy. "Wonder who done it?"

Pollard was grunting under Tom's weight. He twisted an upward look at the crowd. "Any one of you could've done it. I expect there's probably a pretty fair price on his hide by now." He straightened up with an effort. "Come on, dammit, lift, don't drag."

"He's heavier'n a horse-mule, Sheriff," said a man in grunting protest.

"Well, what'd you expect? Feller's got as

much money as he has, eats good an' eats regular."

Eleven men trouped up the hotel stairway to Tom's room. Sheriff Pollard stopped all but those carrying Tom with a scowl at the door. "Go on," he rasped. "Go wet your fangs."

They put Tom on his bed. Pollard dismissed the remaining two men and closed the door behind them. Then he removed Tom's gun, hat, and coat, opened his shirt, and bent forward, squinting at the hole in his chest. "My, my," he said aloud, but softly. "That bushwhacker was a fair to middlin' shot at that, what with there bein' shadows an' all. He only missed by about six inches."

Dr. Spence entered, methodically removed his derby, pursed his lips, and advanced upon the bed. The sheriff moved back.

"Right through the lights," he said.

"I got eyes, Tim."

"Humph!"

"Get the clerk to send up some hot water."

Sheriff Pollard went to the door, opened it, and bawled out for hot water. He closed the door and went back over to watch the doctor work.

"Went clean through him, Tim."

"I know."

Spence straightened up. "Who did it?"

"Dunno. He was a fair shot, though, wouldn't you say?"

Dr. Spence's neck swelled. "No I wouldn't say," he snapped. "When the day arrives that people look on shooting more as a crime than a test of marksmanship, this country'll be a lot better off."

"Uhn-huh. The judge's been talkin' about an ordinance against firearms in town."

"Fat lot of good that'll do, what with the high-powered rifles they make nowadays. Dammit, what's holding up that water anyway?"

"I'll go see, Doc. You just simmer down."

Spence tossed aside his coat, rolled up his sleeves, and bent over the unconscious man. Pollard returned with the water, a clean basin, and several old towels. "Everybody's talkin' about it, Doc," he said, drawing forward a table and filling the basin.

"They have to talk about something, don't they?"

"What I meant was, I got to leave you for a while."

"Why?"

"Trouble. It isn't that folks care about Barker gettin' shot. They just don't approve of bushwhacking."

"Who're they after? Dammit, light the

lamp, Tim."

Sheriff Pollard put the lamp on the table and canted the mantle so the doctor could see. "Clint Ingersoll. How's that?"

"Fine."

"*Adiós,* Doc."

Spence grunted. When he was alone, he worked faster. Finally he drew back, examined his handiwork, went to his coat, withdrew a pony of bourbon, drank deeply, and coughed. "There, Mister Mysterious Barker, you'll probably live . . . only I'm not sure you ought to, after what you did to Moses."

Tom spoke in a quiet tone and Spence's eyes popped wide open. "What did I do to Moses, Doc?"

Spence pushed the bottle into his coat quickly and cleared his throat. "Mustn't talk yet," he admonished. "You got a bad thing there."

"What'd I do to Beach?"

"Well, he had a stroke, didn't he?"

"You think I'm a magician, Doc?"

"Mister Barker, I was there when he came around and started talking. I know what you did. He told me."

"And that's what caused his stroke?"

"I would say it was, yes."

"Then he's got only himself to blame,

Spence. He's the one who wanted to bust Gerald Finnerty so bad he got greedy. It wasn't me. I just came along in time to help a hard-working man keep what's his."

Dr. Spence had fully recovered from the shock of hearing a man he had thought totally unconscious speak to him. "No more talking," he ordered. "That ball pierced your lung. You've got to lie perfectly still and be absolutely quiet for at least a month."

"A month. You're crazy, Doc."

"Am I? Then go ahead and get up, and bleed to death internally. It's your life. Damned if I care what you do with it."

Spence was donning his coat when Tom said: "Who did it?"

"Tim Pollard said a bushwhacker."

"Of course it was a bushwhacker," the man on the bed said impatiently. "If he'd been out in the open, I'd have seen him. But who was he?"

"Don't know yet." Spence picked up his hat, his bag, and crossed to the door. "I'll look at you a little later. Lie still and be quiet."

Tom waited until the door closed, then explored the bandaging with his right hand. He felt slightly feverish but aside from that there was no sensation of illness or shock, not even a headache.

Daylight waned beyond the window. By turning his head to the left he could see the darkening sky. Below him, Beatty was turning quiet; it was the supper hour. A soft knock echoed from the door.

"Come in," he said softly, and raised his head.

"Tom! We just heard."

She floated across the room. Lamplight made her large eyes smoky in the shadows; it reflected off a rapid pulse in the V of her throat.

"You shouldn't have come here," he said, feeling more than uncomfortable, feeling strangely guilty of something.

She drew up a chair, sat down, and took his hand in both hers. "If I didn't come, Tom, who would?"

He heard the reproach and steeled himself to ignore it.

"Didn't you have any warning?"

"None," he said shortly, looking out the window at the sky.

"But you think you know who did it, don't you?"

His eyes swiveled to her face. "I think I know all right, Toni. Want me to tick 'em off for you? Pollard, Clint Ingersoll, the judge, Elihu Gorman. . . ."

"How can you say that!" She let go of his hand.

He watched redness fill her cheeks and under other circumstances he might have smiled. "They're the ones who'd like to have done it, Toni. But a couple of them haven't got the guts."

She was staring into his eyes with her back rigid and her mouth thinned out by disapproval. Suddenly she said: "I shouldn't have come."

"That's right . . . you shouldn't have. But since you did come, tell me something. Does the judge want his twenty tons of hay at eleven dollars yet?"

She had control of herself now, but the smokiness remained in her eyes. He thought he saw a sob tear at her throat and looked quickly away.

"Tom, please. . . ."

"You'd best go, Toni."

"I'm not ready to go yet. Look at me, Tom." His head did not move on the pillow; his dark stare was stonily fixed on the brightening stars beyond the window. "Tom . . . ?"

"Listen to me, Toni. Last night you practically called me. . . ."

"That was last night. You're hurt now."

"Nothing's changed. I'll be up and around

again in a few days." He faced her with a quick turn of his head. "Toni, I can't change. I came here for a purpose. I'm going to stay until I do it. Do you understand me?"

"I understood you last night, Tom. I know what you're here to do. Ruin Mister Beach and drive the judge out of the livery business. And there'll be others, too, won't there?"

"Yes."

She drew back in the chair. Her body softened and settled lower. After a time she said: "Is it completely useless to try and reason with you, Tom? Are you that far gone?"

"I think so, yes."

She got up suddenly, stood there gazing down at the bed. "Can I get you anything?"

"Yes. Please hand me my gun." When she had complied, he said — "Thank you." — without looking up at her.

"Shall I send up something to eat, Tom?"

"I'm not hungry, thanks."

"Tom . . .?"

"Good night, Toni."

"No," she said in a voice that had to be swift to be steady, "not good night. Good bye!"

The pain started then. He could feel it

spiraling upward and locked his jaws against it. It pulsed in cadence to her steps as long as he could distinguish them, and continued in the same way when he no longer could.

The hours passed. Dr. Spence came and went; they exchanged no more than ten words. Spence was gruff and Tom was silent. Down below in the road he heard riders jingling past, their light, carefree voices raised in merriment. Nostalgia touched him; it had been good to ride into a town like that, full of laughter and thirst and sticky with sweat. Then he heard booted feet slamming up the stairs two at a time, ringing spurs mingling in their echo. The door burst open and Tex stood framed in the opening, eyes wide with disbelief.

"Hell, Tom. We just heard . . . out at the ranch. You going to make it?"

"I'll make it. When're you and Finnerty taking that drive out?"

"Finnerty, pardner, not me. You need a nursemaid."

"Like hell I do."

"Well, now," Tex said, straddling the chair Toni had vacated and grinning from ear to ear. "Like hell you don't. But do or don't, you got one. Want to jump up and whip me so's I'll go away?" When Tom glared in deep silence, Tex's grin threatened to tear his face. "Just what I thought. Can't do it, can you?"

XII

Tom earned Albigence Spence's eternal disapproval by walking down to the Queens & Aces Café nine days after he had been shot, and eating a steak breakfast. But his arrival at the Royal Antler Saloon to some extent ameliorated Spence's dire prophecies; there, he was greeted with broad smiles and congratulations by men he knew only by sight. He bought a round of drinks, sat for a while at the wall table, then crossed the road to Pollard's office.

"You know who did it, Sheriff?" he asked.

Pollard eyed him laconically and said: "Nope. There's more'n one would like to see you dead. I don't know which one to start with."

"Ingersoll?"

"I talked to him. I don't figure Clint's a good enough actor to fool me. He swore he didn't do it. He also said he wished he had . . . only he didn't shoot from hiding."

"I believe that," Tom agreed.

"He also told me about your fight."

"Well?"

"Nothing. Just proves I'm right. I said

Clint wasn't a bushwhacker. I told the crowd that the night you got shot. I was right about another thing, too."

"I'm listening."

"You aren't out to kill anyone for the hell of it."

Tom turned toward the door. "You're getting wiser by the minute, Sheriff."

"Just a second!" Pollard called. "You've been out of circulation a few days. I've been learnin' things about you in that time."

"Go on," said Tom, leaning on the door.

"You got Moses. You about got the judge. Elihu Gorman wasn't around when you was a kid here in Beatty, but you've got him eatin' out of your hand, too. That leaves only me." Pollard's steady faded stare lingered on the younger man. "When you goin' to call me out, boy?"

"Would you come?" Tom countered.

The sheriff considered this through an interval of silence. Then he drew up in his chair. "I reckon I would. I wouldn't want to, not over anything as silly as what's eatin' you, Tom, but I would if I had to."

"I'll let you know," Barker said, and walked back out into the sunlight.

He was heading for the bank when Dr. Spence came floating across the road from the Royal Antler. He was moving with the immense and solid dignity of a drunken man who was concentrating very hard on walking erect and straight. "*Ah,* Barker," he intoned with greater irony than Tom would have thought anyone in his condition capable of, "the damned walking dead, eh?"

Tom would have moved past but only the infirmity of his prolonged siege with a bed was bothering him now — weak legs.

"You are a fool," Spence said, squinting upward. "A fool and a hero, eh? Not afraid. No, sir, you are not afraid he will return for another try . . . and that's why you are a fool. Of course he will try again. He didn't get caught, did he?" The doctor's squint spread over his entire screwed-up face. "A fool, a hero, a rugged physical specimen, but more than any of those things, you are a fine hater." Spence swiped at his damp forehead. "Do you know what a hater is, Barker? No? Well, I'll tell you. It's a man without reason. No reasoning animal hates as deeply and for as long a time as you have. No reasoning animal . . . but you aren't a reasoning animal, are you? You're a cold, merciless, unreasoning hater."

"You're drunk," Tom said coldly.

Spence absorbed this philosophically. "Of course I'm drunk. Why shouldn't I be? I studied nine years to become a great surgeon and I've spent thirty years in this infernal country digging bullets out of people. I've wasted an entire human lifetime, digging bullets out of carcasses so damned ignorant . . . most of 'em . . . that they couldn't even write their own names. Of course I'm drunk." The doctor looked around for something to lean against or sit upon, found nothing, and faced Tom again, weaving a little from side to side. "You want me to unbosom myself, as they say in the theater?"

"No."

"Well, I'm going to anyway, my boy. I'm going to anyway." He drew in a big breath and exhaled it slowly. He squared his shoulders and threw back his head. "I'm going to tell you something you don't know, big man. I'm going to watch you shrink down to my size."

Tom's legs felt better; he started past. Dr. Spence reached out and caught him in a tight grip.

"Just a minute, Barker. I'm going to tell you this if it's the last damned thing I ever do."

"Take your hand off my arm, Doctor, or it just might be the last thing you ever do."

"Ho!" Spence hooted. "You'd shoot me, would you?" But he removed his hand. Then his face smoothed out and his eyes burned with a strange and sardonic light. "You recollect the night your mother left this damned town, Barker?"

Tom made no reply. His mouth turned slowly flat and dangerous-looking.

"I see you remember all right," Spence said, grinning. "Know what I think? That's mostly what's eating at your innards. Well, let me tell you something about that. . . ."

"Doc!"

Sheriff Pollard's voice cracked like a whip. Dr. Spence started, turned his head to watch the lawman come up, then, without another word, he started away from Tom. Just before he turned down an alley, he halted, looked back, drew himself up, and squared his shoulders, then passed from sight between two buildings. Tom's throat felt as though it was full of ashes.

"He gets kind of windy every once in a while," Pollard remarked, stopping to face Tom, his voice back to normal. "Too bad. I expect that's why he hangs on here 'stead of going back East where the money is."

Tom's black stare was unwavering and knife-sharp. "Why'd you shut him up like that?" he demanded.

"*Pshaw,* boy, he was makin' a spectacle of himself, bein' drunk an' disorderly."

"It was more than that, Sheriff."

Pollard's inscrutably squinted eyes remained mild. "Naw," he protested. "What else could it have been?"

"Whatever he was on the verge of telling me."

Pollard shook his head without speaking, and Tom, studying his face, came to the slow realization that Tim Pollard would never tell anything he did not want to tell. He turned abruptly away and resumed his way toward the bank.

Elihu Gorman was not in. There was another man waiting to see him; it was Judge Montgomery and he looked annoyed. When he saw Tom enter the building, he snapped at a clerk: "Tell him I want to see him this evening."

Tom watched the judge depart, then collared the same clerk. "Gorman in?"

"No, sir. He went out into the country. I don't think he'll be back until pretty late."

"Tell him Tom Barker wants to see him."

"Yes, sir."

Once more on the plank walk, Tom met Tex. They spoke together briefly, and Tex was starting away, toward the livery stable, when three unkempt men came out of a saddle and boot shop nearby. Tex swung wide to avoid a collision and noticed only that they were freighters. He would normally have forgotten them but one made a grunt at sight of Tom and sang out unpleasantly: "The big man himself."

Tex turned. He could see Tom's face over the head of the shortest, thickest of the freighters. It was white to the eyes.

"Come ridin' out o' nowhere," the freighter went on. "Come ridin' into Beatty plumb loaded down with money. Goin' t'be top lash. *Hah!*"

The tallest of the three freighters was Clinton Ingersoll. He stood slouched now, one hand hanging free, the other hand hooked in his shell belt. He was smiling with naked hatred in each line of his face. But it was neither Clint nor the other young freighter who spoke; it was the grizzled older man between them. "Top lash o' Beatty. . . ."

Tom started to turn away. Six feet behind the freighters Tex was rooted to the ground. He had never before seen dark Tom Barker walk away from a fight, and it was very clear the freighters were enjoying his discomfort immensely. It was also clear to Tex that their intention was to force a fight.

"Hey, big man," the grizzled freighter said. "Where you goin'?"

Tom made no answer, but continued to

move off.

Clint Ingersoll spoke one word then: "Bastard."

Tex's eyes sprang wide. Tom was turning; the whiteness of his face let that one word sink into dead silence.

"Go ahead," Ingersoll said, his meaning very clear.

Tex flexed his gun hand while the stillness ran on. The freighters in front of him, concentrating their full attention upon Tom, were oblivious to the danger in their rear. Tom was not going to fight. Tex could see that. He was not even going to speak. Tex's mouth went dry with distaste; anger burned in him. He said very thinly: "Turn around, Ingersoll. I'll oblige you."

The grizzled freighter's shoulders stiffened but he made no move. The other, younger man, licked his lips, the light of battle dying in his eyes. Clint turned slowly.

"Any time," Tex said, and, when Ingersoll made no move, his lips curled in scorn. "Big talk, Ingersoll. Big talk when you figured it'd be three to one. Go ahead, make your play."

Ingersoll stood erect, his jaw hard-set and grim. He was not a fast-thinking man and this situation was something he could not cope with — a fast gun behind him, another fast gun in front of him. If he got one, he could not hope to get the other one. He licked his lips, the decision forced upon him. "I got no fight with you," he said.

"Well, now," Tex replied sardonically, seeing it plain in Ingersoll's face that he was not going to go for his gun. "That's where you're wrong. I'm a mite partial to that name you called Tom Barker. I just naturally figure to fight whenever I hear it, Ingersoll."

"I wasn't talkin' to you, feller."

"Don't mean nothin', Ingersoll. Like I said, I'm just plain partial to that word."

"I won't draw," Ingersoll said hoarsely.

"Why then I expect I'll just kill you anyway . . . you yellow swine!"

Tom was moving forward; he stopped close to Clint Ingersoll, his hand moved down and up, and Ingersoll's gun thudded across the plank walk into the roadway. Tex straightened up very slowly, face reddening. He looked squarely at Tom, saying nothing. Now the other two freighters turned to look at Tex, and Tom disarmed them the same way.

"No fight, Tex. Come on."

The freighters continued to stare at Tex as though imprinting his features upon their memories. The older man was a vicious and dissolute-looking person. Tex had seen murder in men's eyes before and he recognized it now.

"Better give 'em back their guns, Tom," he said past stiff lips. "I ain't like you. I ain't goin' to give 'em a second chance to kill me."

Tom prodded the freighters. "Go on," he said. "Move off and don't stop."

Ingersoll led out, imminent peril sharpening his perception. The other two men followed him in stony silence. Tom watched them go along the walk as far as the Mexican café on the west side of the road and turn in there, then he finally relaxed.

Tex, round eyes speculative, lingered a moment waiting for the distance between them to be broken. When it was not, when it became hard to bear, he struck out for the Queens & Aces Café without a backward glance. He knew Tom was still standing there by the boot and saddle shop, looking into the glittering daylight.

"Excuse me."

Tex's head jerked up. "Ma'am," he said harshly, avoiding a collision, but still moving.

"Sir . . . ?"

He stopped, focused his eyes with an effort and touched his hat unconsciously. It was the handsome girl he'd seen Tom walk away from the dance with. The girl Tom'd kissed in the shadows of the old cottonwood tree. The judge's daughter.

"I saw what happened over there," she said, looking squarely into his face.

"Did you, ma'am?"

"You're a friend of Tom Barker's." She saw the shadow cloud his vision. "I think I know what you're thinking."

He was icily polite. "Do you, ma'am?"

"You're thinking he lost his nerve, that he was afraid to fight them."

Tex remained silent, looking down into her face with his bleak expression.

"But there is something you don't know. Something that was happening over there that goes back many years."

Much of the hostility left him; he slouched; he even smiled slightly at her. His condescension annoyed her; he saw that, too, in the smoky flare of her glance. "Ma'am," he said quietly, "a feller calls you a name like that, you fight. It don't matter what else there is, you fight."

She turned ironic. "Do you indeed? Would you have killed all three of them?"

"The odds don't mean nothing, ma'am. You fight, that's all there is to it."

"Even," she said slowly, "if one of those men is your father?"

XIII

Tom was lying on his bed staring at the ceiling when Elihu Gorman knocked on the door. He called for him to enter and sat up.

"Good evening," the banker said.

Tom nodded, ran a hand through his hair, and motioned for the banker to be seated.

"You wanted to see me?"

"Yeah. Where you been all day, Gorman?"

Elihu would have resented Tom's question and tone if he had dared to, but he did not; he had just come from a bitter visit with Judge Montgomery. "Out in the country," he replied.

"Looking for hay?"

"What?"

"Looking for hay for the judge?"

"Well," Gorman said a little breathlessly, "why would I be doing that, Mister Barker?"

Tom leaned back, gazed briefly out at the settling night, then turned a worn and tired expression toward the banker. "Because you need his friendship, Gorman, that's why."

"Of course his friendship is valuable," the banker retorted with some heat. "He's one of our more substantial citizens, Mister Barker."

"So you were out looking for hay for him."

Gorman reddened. "See here, Mister Barker. . . ."

Tom made a tired gesture. "Cut it out, Gorman. You got forty thousand dollars from the judge to buy Finnerty's mortgage from the bank. You engineered Finnerty's foreclosure. You had it all set up to resell Finnerty's place to Evan Houston, the biggest cowman in these parts."

Elihu's working face was pale; his eyes were round and fearful.

"And you've got to get the judge to go along with you because you can't repay the loan and interest on time." Tom took out his tobacco sack, considered it a moment, then returned it to his pocket. Although he felt fine, his lung was not yet healed. As he went on speaking, though, the longing for a smoke persisted.

"That's the secured loan you talked to me about. You figured if you could get forty thousand from me for two years at low interest, the worst that would happen would be that you and Moses could pay it off. On the other hand, if anything happened to Gerald Finnerty in those two years, you could still get his ranch, sell it to Houston, make your big profit, and still come out smelling like roses." Tom's expression hardened. His steady stare remained on the banker's face. "If anything happens to Finnerty, Gorman, you're not going to be around to make any big deal with Houston."

"Barker. . . ."

"Shut up and listen."

Gorman subsided. He was sitting very erect in the chair.

"Did you get the hay?"

No answer.

"Did you get the hay?"

"No," Gorman breathed softly, "no, I did not."

"Couldn't scare anyone into selling?"

"I didn't try to scare them, Barker."

"Of course you didn't," said Tom dourly. "The local banker drives up. Any cowman who has ever borrowed money from you or thinks he might have to someday begins to sweat. You didn't have to scare them, did you?"

Gorman was thinking. His face gradually resumed its normal expression. He cleared his throat and spread both hands out toward Tom. "Barker, you want to make money and so do I. I'll tell you how it can be done. Big money, Barker."

"I'm listening."

"You have Finnerty's note."

"Go on."

"You can use it as leverage to get his ranch."

"And?"

"I've got Evan Houston all ready to buy the Finnerty place at seventy-five thousand dollars cash." Gorman leaned back, watching Tom's face. He could tell nothing from the blank expression, nor from the unwavering dark eyes. The silence ran on; Gorman began to squirm on his chair. "Well?"

"I'll tell you a better way to get out from under your trouble, Gorman. Get a bill of sale to Moses Beach's store and use it as collateral for borrowing more money."

"How would that help?"

"It wouldn't help you, Gorman, but it'd sure help me." Tom straightened up on the bed. "I want Beach's scalp, Gorman. I also want Judge Montgomery's scalp. The only thing I've got against you is that you're on their side of the fence. You can break Beach with a note on his store."

"But. . . ."

"Listen, Gorman, you keep on crossing me for those two and you're going to wind up pretty badly used up." The banker started to arise. Tom stopped him with a gesture. "I spotted you for a worse crook than a stage robber the first time we met. What you just suggested I do to Gerald

Finnerty clinches it for me. Now, I'm going to give you a choice of leaving Beatty on the next stage or of getting called out the next time we meet."

Gorman sprang to his feet, eyes blazing. "You're a fool and an idiot, Barker. Moses Beach told me all about you."

"That shouldn't have taken him long," Tom replied dryly, also arising. "All that he remembers was that he wouldn't help a little kid because it might've interfered with his storekeeping." Tom reached out and tapped Gorman on the chest with his finger. The banker backed quickly away, not from the finger but from the strange, black light in the big man's eyes. "Gorman, you're a pretty good shot for a banker. I owe you something for that and I believe in paying my debts."

"What are you talking about?"

Tom's hand dropped to his side. "This bandage I got under my shirt."

"You're crazy, Barker."

"Gorman, the judge wouldn't have done it. Moses Beach couldn't have done it. Sheriff Pollard came up from the south of town a minute after I went down, but the bullet that hit me came from around a building to the north. That leaves you."

"It does not. It leaves Clint Ingersoll."

Tom shook his head. "I've met Ingersoll twice. Both times he could've bushwhacked me easy. He didn't. He isn't the bushwhacking kind. You are, Gorman. Now tell me why you tried it?"

The banker retreated as far as the door and put a hand behind him. Tom crossed the room swiftly toward him. Gorman ducked away, breathing heavily. Tom stopped suddenly, his right arm swinging, hovering above the gun he wore. Gorman bleated: "I'm unarmed, Barker!"

"You won't be when the sheriff finds you."

"Barker, hell. . . ."

"Why, Gorman?"

"It was Moses's idea."

"I'll bet."

"I swear it, Barker. He said you'd ruined us by backing Finnerty, that you wouldn't stop there, and that you had to be put out of the way."

Tom walked to the chair Gorman had vacated and sank down. He did not look at the banker. "Get out, Gorman. Get out and remember what I told you. Be on the evening stage out of Beatty or I'm going to kill you."

The banker left.

Tom got up finally, crossed to the window, and looked out at the night. It was hot out;

there was not the slightest hint of a breeze. His room was like a furnace. Below the window two men were talking. One he recognized as Tim Pollard; the other man was deep in shadow and murkily silhouetted. The longing for a smoke came back stronger than ever. He reached for his coat, shrugged into it, and left the room. He went out into the night, moved along the walk, sniffing the air and reaching with his eyes for movement. Pollard was still across the road, sitting now, on a bench outside the jailhouse, whittling a stick that shone dimly white in the gloom. He looked up when Tom approached, his knife hanging in the air, then he resumed his whittling. Tom sat, pushed his legs out, and sighed.

"Hot," Pollard opined.

Tom ignored it. Around him Beatty lay in soft shadow, gentled by it.

"Your pardner's over at the Royal Antler."

Fishing, Tom thought. *The old devil's heard about Tex and me and now he's curious.*

"Guess he gave you a bad start today. Him an' your paw."

Like an old Indian squaw, always seemingly indifferent, disinterested, and lazing around, but missing nothing, Tom watched two riders enter town from the west in a tight lope side-by-side, swerve in at the

Royal Antler, and swing down.

"He come in with that latest train of wagons, Tom. If I'd've known, I'd've told you."

Busybody, Tom thought. *Why would he have told me my father had returned to Beatty? What business was it of his?* "You trying to soften me up, Sheriff?" he asked finally. "Because if you are, save it."

Shavings fell, pale and curled and pine-scented. "I reckon you don't know me so well, after all," Pollard retorted quietly. "I'm not the blarneyin' kind. Never have been." Shavings continued to peel off and tumble to the ground. "And maybe I don't know you so well, either."

"Meaning?"

The knife snapped closed, went into a Levi's pocket, and Tim Pollard stood up. "Care to walk a piece with me?" he asked.

Tom cocked his head back. "To where?"

"Just walk. Not far, boy. Exercise'll do you good."

Tom stood and considered the craggy old face, then they moved off together. For a while Sheriff Pollard contented himself with saying nothing. Finally he opened up again. "Doc Spence left town last night."

Tom felt surprise rise in him. He went back over his last meeting with the medical man. "Why?" he asked.

"Just up and left. Didn't even come by and tell me s'long."

"If he's gone, maybe you won't mind telling me why you shut him up the other night, Sheriff."

Pollard evidently had given this much thought, for now he had a ready answer. "Some things a feller knows that don't come easy to say, boy."

"Then you *did* shut him up?"

"We both know that," the sheriff said simply.

They came to the end of the plank walk. Beyond, stretching inkily to invisible bald hills, lay the northward plains.

"Are you going to tell me, or aren't you?" Tom demanded.

Pollard teetered on the walkway, gazing outward. "I'd rather not, Tom. It won't do no good to tell you." He stepped down off the last plank into the dust and turned westerly. "Come along. It isn't much farther."

"What isn't?"

But Tim Pollard trudged along in total silence, shoulders bowed forward and eyes fixed on something neither of them could see, but which they both knew lay just beyond town within its rusting, sagging iron fence. Beatty's cemetery.

When the sheriff stopped, put out a hand and closed his fingers around an iron paling, Tom also halted. He had that peculiar taste of ashes in his throat again. Something darkly, instinctively knowing was working in his mind.

"Ever been here before, Tom?"

"When I was a kid, yes."

"Lots of folks buried here. Lately, when I've followed the hearse out here, I've had the feelin' I know more of these folks than the ones back in town." Pollard twisted to gaze at him. "When a feller gets to feeling that way, I expect he's about at the end of his rope. He's gettin' pretty damned old."

Tom's eyes were accustomed to the darkness. Beyond the iron fence he could discern headstones and, occasionally, forlorn little tins with dead flowers in them. "Does this have something to do with what you don't want to tell me?" he asked.

The lawman nodded. "Yes, and like I said . . . there's things better left unsaid." He straightened up a little, gazing at the dry, flinty earth. "You still bent on knowing, Tom?"

"I am."

Sheriff Pollard's eyes went to one stone and remained there. He seemed to be selecting words. "That grave yonder, boy, the one with the little pillow-like stone, you see it?"

"I see it." Tom's voice had sunk to a whisper. The thing in his mind was taking on form, substance, solidity; it was becoming a premonition with shape and meaning. "I see it, Sheriff."

"That's your mother, son. She's restin' there."

"That's what Spence was going to tell me?"

"That's part of it, Tom."

"Then why did you shut him up?"

Sheriff Pollard put both hands out, curled them around cold iron, and leaned a little forward. "What's the use, Tom? She's gone. You recollect her one way. That's the way you should always remember her, son."

"Tell me the rest of it."

"All right," Tim Pollard said gently. "She come back to Beatty the year after you run off. She was sick, Tom, had lung fever. Doc did everything he could for her. . . ."

"Doc Spence?"

"Yes. This is the part it'd've been better left unsaid, Tom. Doc was in love with your maw. He kept her at his house for a year an' your paw never knew. . . ."

"Then she died?"

"Then she died, and he buried her here." The lawman narrowed his eyes. "There's only her first name on that stone. Doc didn't want your paw to know, naturally."

"Why did she come back, Sheriff?"

"To get you and take you away. But you was gone and no one ever heard of you again until the day you come ridin' in a couple months back, Tom."

"And . . . the man she ran off with?"

But the sheriff straightened up and dusted off his palms. "Doc never asked and she never said. What's the difference?"

"There's no difference, I guess."

"No. Your mother was a fine woman, Tom. Don't you ever doubt it or forget it." The lawman was turning away.

"One more thing," Tom said to him. "Did you know Doc Spence was hiding her?"

"I knew. Doc and I were sort of close. There's another thing too, Tom. Your paw made her life hell on earth. That doesn't give you no call to hunt him down . . . and believe me, boy, she wouldn't have wanted you to do that. I know."

"How do you know?"

"She an' Doc an' me used to sit on his back porch that last summer, in the evenings, and sort of talk."

"I see." Tom also turned away from the

iron fence. "Now tell me the end of it. Why did Spence leave Beatty?"

Sheriff Pollard shrugged as they strolled back toward town. "Who knows why folks do things? Maybe it was seein' you. Maybe you opened an old wound in him. Maybe he just couldn't stand Beatty any more. All I know for certain is what the stage driver told me. He bought a ticket to Saint Joe, Missouri."

XIV

Tom did not sleep in his hotel room that night. He took two blankets, got his horse, and rode up into the hills. He spread one blanket on the dry forage grass by the little creek where he and Tex often met, lay down, and draped the upper blanket over his body. The last echoes of movement died around him, the moon-shot blackness and the deep hush of late night closed down, and mystery trembled in the windless night while he breathed an incensed air. Overhead, glittering in their purple setting, an immense diadem of diamonds shone down. To the motionless man whose black eyes were dull but sleepless, they seemed to turn soft, like a woman's tears.

It was a long night and it held no surcease

for him. He did not sleep until shortly before the east was streaked with pale pink, and even then he slept so lightly that the sound of a horse's shod hoof striking stone brought him fully awake.

"Howdy, Tom," Tex said, dismounting. "Figured you might be up here." He flung down saddlebags and began grubbing for twigs. When he had built the tiny, pointed range-man's cooking fire, he rummaged through the saddlebags for his dented, black coffee pan, filled it with water, then sat back watching flames lick and curl beneath it.

"This isn't Monday," Tom said gruffly, sitting upright.

"It ain't Friday, either," Tex said imperturbably, pouring ground coffee sparingly into the water and wrinkling his nose. "Nothing on this earth smells as good as cooking coffee. Too bad it doesn't taste as good as it smells."

Tex sat back, made a cigarette, smoked a moment with obvious pleasure, then brought forth three cups that he swabbed out carefully with grass switches, and lined up one beside the other. Tom watched this briefly, then got up, went down to the creek, washed, combed his hair, and came stamping back. He dropped down, crossed his legs, and regarded the three tin cups. "You going to drink two at a time?" he asked grumpily.

Tex smoked a moment longer before he replied. "Nope, we got company."

The dark eyes raised swiftly. "Who?"

"More'n one."

"Who, damn you?"

"Better mind your language," Tex said, unruffled, then raised his voice. "Coffee's on, ladies."

Tom turned. They emerged from the willows south of where he'd washed, side-by-side — Miss Eloise and Toni Montgomery. He felt like swearing, or jumping up and leaving, or even striking Tex. Instead, he sat there watching Toni move toward him. She was wearing a split riding skirt and a very white blouse. Her hair was caught up at the base of her neck and held in place by a small blue ribbon. She looked fresh and cool and lovely. The rising heat of the new day seemed not to affect her and its reflection from her blouse was painful to his eyes. Eloise smiled into his face, her violet gaze dancing, but Toni only nodded and passed him, stopping beside Tex who held up a cup.

"Thank you, Tex."

The words jarred Tom out of his silence. He took the cup Tex offered and hunkered, not looking in Toni's direction at all.

Eloise sat down and looked quickly at the others. Of them all she was the least affected by undercurrents. "Any sugar?" she asked sweetly of Tex.

"Never use the stuff," Tex said, darted a look at Tom, and stubbed out his cigarette. "Sit down, Miss Toni." She sat. Tex drew in a big breath. "Tom," he said, speaking clearly and as though he had rehearsed what he was saying, "Finnerty's back. Came in about dawn on the stage."

"Yeah?"

"Yeah. He's got your loan money, too."

"All right. I'll look him up when I go back to town."

"Something else," Tex said. "That banker left town last night."

"Did he now?"

Toni squirmed. Tom sensed rather than saw it. "My father has taken over the bank, Tom," she informed him. "Temporarily, until someone else can be appointed to Elihu Gorman's position."

Tom blew into the steam arising from his cup. "That's fine. The best man in town for the job."

"I'm glad you think so."

"No question about it."

"Tom . . . ?"

"Yes'm."

"Dammit, look up when I'm talking to you."

The profanity startled all of them. Tex looked at her with his lower lip hanging. Eloise was round-eyed, and Tom's head sprang up.

"That's better," said Antoinette, her voice going soft and rich again. "There is a forty thousand dollar note at the bank with your signature on it."

Tom was crouched like a stone image staring at her. He put aside the cup of coffee very slowly. "What do you mean?"

"The judge found it this morning."

"I never gave any such note, Toni."

"Of course you didn't. That's what Tex said when I told him. That's why we three are up here this morning." Some of her spirit showed in the gray eyes. "Otherwise I wouldn't be here at all . . . regardless of what Tex or Tim Pollard said."

"What did they say?" he demanded.

"It doesn't matter. What matters is that your signature is on that note to the bank."

"Are you telling me I owe the bank in Beatty forty thousand dollars, Toni?"

She nodded.

Tom looked at Tex and spoke a name: "Gorman?" Tex nodded. Tom stood up. "I see. That's paying me back."

"Huh?"

"Nothing."

"Where are you going?"

"After him."

"Wait." Tex was on his feet. "You won't get a mile down the road. Not unless you listen first."

"Why not?"

Toni and Eloise also got to their feet. "Because my father and Tim Pollard have posses out looking for you, Tom," Toni said.

This was something he hadn't considered. Now he said: "Are you saying that Gorman actually took forty thousand dollars of the bank's money and left that note he'd forged?"

"Yes. And the judge believes you're fleeing with the money."

"No, I don't believe he really thinks that, Toni. I think your father sees his chance for hitting back and he's doing it this way."

She flushed scarlet and for a moment he thought her wrath was going to break out. He was bracing into it when she regained control and spoke in an icy voice: "He'd have reason to believe that, the way you've acted since you've returned, Tom. But Eloise and Tex and I think we can prove to him it was Gorman and not you who took the money."

"How?" he demanded.

Tex fished a paper and pencil from a pocket and shoved them at Tom. "Write your name on there like you always write it."

"Why?"

"Consarn it! So's we can take it back to the judge and make him compare it with the signature on the note. That's why."

Tom wrote his name and returned the paper and pencil. He was nodding. "Sure, and here's something else, too," He gave them the creased note he and Gerald Finnerty had signed. "Give him that, too. It also has my signature on it and it's dated over a month back."

Tex was putting the papers into his pocket when Tom caught his horse and bent to saddling it. As he led the animal forward, he beckoned to Tex. "Fetch your horse. You're going with me. Give the notes to Miss Toni."

Tex obeyed. While he was moving toward his horse to secure the saddlebags and check the cinch, Eloise walked toward him, leaving Toni and Tom Barker facing one another across the smoldering fire. She made a fluttery motion with her hands. "The thing that will save you is that you haven't signed anything back in town."

"Oh?"

"He couldn't have known what your signature looked like, Tom."

He looked grimly at her. "That's not the only thing that's going to save me. Gorman's going to help, too."

"What if you don't find him, Tom?"

He mounted and gazed down from the saddle. "I'll find him. I'll find him and fetch him back."

"Tom . . . ?"

"Yes'm."

"Can I ask a favor of you?"

"I owe you that much, Toni."

"Let me tell Gerald Finnerty it's all right to sell twenty tons of hay to my father."

He lingered a moment to look into her face, then he shook his head negatively, spun his horse, and rode off. Tex, mounted and looking on, stifled a curse and shook a fist at Tom's retreating back. "Ma'am," he said to Toni, "this'll likely take some riding. You just hang and rattle. I'll have his harness shook out, talked out, or kicked out, by the time we get back. You go ahead and tell Finnerty it's all right to bring in that hay."

But Toni was standing as though she hadn't heard, watching Tom lope northward toward the far lift and fall of a side hill.

Tex caught Tom on the downward side of the hill and slowed beside him. He made no mention of what was uppermost in his mind, but said instead: "He's got a long start on us."

Tom made no answer. He jogged along, gazing ahead at the unfolding plains coming up the hill to meet them, the sun-dried floor, the faint gray of banks where winter's deluges had scored the shifting earth, the faint showings of shadows under brush and rocks, and farther out like a flung-down old snake the roadway leading north.

"Of course, since he's traveling on coaches, we'll make faster time."

"And if he went south instead of north?" Tom asked dryly.

But Tex knew as well as did Tom that the night stage out of Beatty only went one way — north. He looped the reins and began manufacturing a cigarette. "You're sure hep for arguments today, aren't you?"

No reply. The road shimmered and writhed and the heat increased. There was no depth to the distance, only a pale, bright yellowness.

"If I had your conscience, I'd feel meaner'n poison, too," Tex opined, inhaling and exhaling. "Funny how some fellers are, Tom. Mean inside and not really very mean-looking on the outside." He inspected the cigarette, knocked off gray ash with his little finger, and took up the reins again in his left hand. "And when they really got no reason to be, too."

"Why don't you shut up?"

Tex became silent.

They rode as hard as they dared in that glaring and waterless expanse, saving their horses when they could, taking time when it was safe to do so, and at sunset the village of Mirage appeared dead ahead. They refilled their canteens, had their horses washed down, grained, and watered, then struck out again, riding through the hot but pleasant night side-by-side.

"Feller at the stage station said it was him, all right," Tex reported. "Said we'd catch 'em if we stayed with it all night, more'n likely."

They stayed with it all night, riding more swiftly as the coolness increased, confident in both their hearts they would catch Elihu Gorman, but beyond that thinking differently. Tex thought Tom would probably kill him. He didn't think he should because the absconding banker was the only one who could clear him before Judge Montgomery. But on the other hand — they were riding the turn-outs in the high north country, and, if he killed the banker, they could just keep on riding, get clear of all this dirt and deceit and discomfort. Tex was a simple, laughing man; his vision extended no farther than the next drive, the next hunt, the next ride into strange country.

"Tom?"

"Yeah."

"That was a lousy thing you done to that girl."

Silence.

"You know, she sweated bullets trying to talk her paw into holding off the posses. And you wouldn't even let her have twenty tons of watery old grass hay."

"It's not her, it's her paw."

"You didn't say that, you just shook your head."

Silence.

"Tom?"

"Now what."

"I'm splitting off when we find Gorman. I'm heading back for the high country."

The sun was sending up its pink feelers when they saw the little town huddled against a red-stone hill less than three miles ahead. Sharp new light on wooden fronts and low adobe houses stood out, mingling with shadows. "He'd better be here," Tom said, touching cracked lips with his tongue.

"If he ain't, he rented a horse and went on alone," said Tex. "That stationmaster at Mirage said they lay over here until the southbound morning stage comes in."

They were riding down the empty, dust-layered roadway when Tom pointed. "There's the coach."

"Yep. He'll be asleep at the station probably."

As they dismounted in the still and fragrant coolness, Tom looked across his saddle leather. "Tex? You didn't mean that back there, did you?"

Tex kept his head averted, hitched up his shell belt, and patted his horse. "Damned critter's tucked up like a gutted snowbird," he said, ignoring the question. "Well, let's roust him out."

XV

Tex thought the look on Elihu Gorman's face, when they found him bedded down at the adobe stage station and Tom shook him awake, was almost worth the grueling twenty-hour ride, and, if his stomach hadn't been flap-empty and hung up on his backbone, he might even have smiled. As it was, he simply reached down, grasped Gorman's shoulder, and jerked him upright off the cot, and, when Gorman fumbled under his coat, Tex slapped his wrist hard and the little under-and-over .41 Derringer fell to the earthen floor with scarcely a sound.

Three other sleeping men in the room did not stir. Tex propelled the banker out into the soft dawn light and let go of him when he heard Tom cock his pistol. Gorman's head jerked at the little snippet of mechanical sound; his eyes widened and grew very round; they fixed a watery stare on Tom Barker as Tex moved aside. "No," he croaked. "Wait a minute, Barker . . . I'll return it."

"Where is it?"

The banker worked frantic fingers at his clothing, reached under his shirt, and drew out the money belt and let it fall. Tex retrieved the belt, hefted it, and made a silent whistle with his lips. "Didn't know paper money had so much weight."

Tom eased off the hammer and holstered his gun. "You're a vengeful cuss, aren't you?" he said to Gorman. "Why weren't you satisfied just to take the money?"

Before the banker could respond, Tex cut in with: "Yeah. I got a notion if you'd just taken the money, Tom would've let you go. He don't like Beatty anyway. But feller, when you stuck his name on that note, you invited us to run you down." Tex wagged his head. "That wasn't very smart, Gorman."

"Take half the money and let me go," the banker offered. Then, seeing the mirthless smile on Tex Earle's face, he said: "Take it all. Just let me go."

"You're going, all right," Tom said dryly. "But south, not north."

Gorman shuffled his feet. His sleepy, puffy face turned tense and his eyes moved wetly.

Tom shook his head gently. "Don't try it, Gorman. You wouldn't get fifty feet."

A rumpled-looking man came to the doorway of one of the adobe huts, scratched an ample belly with both hands, made a circuit of the inside of his mouth with his tongue, and spat, squinted long at the rising sun, then, hearing voices, turned and stared, mouth dropping open and bleary eyes widening. He jumped back out of sight and reappeared a moment later with a cocked riot gun in both hands.

"Here!" he called out boomingly. "What'n hell's going on over there?"

Tom eyed the shotgun and the stubbly face above it. "Nothing that concerns you," he retorted. "We're just taking a bank robber back to Beatty."

Acting quickly Elihu called out: "That's a

lie! These two just took my money belt."

Tex, still holding the belt, looked from it to the man with the shotgun. "Hey," he protested, "point that damned thing some other direction, mister. They got a habit of going off."

The shotgun made a tight, short arc. Its holder snarled: "Drop them guns you two, and make no mistake, this thing'll cut you in two at that distance." As Tom and Tex were moving to comply, the stage company hostler raised his voice: "Sam! Oh, Sam! Come out here!"

A second man appeared in the doorway. He was holding a griddle-cake turner in one hand and he was scowling darkly, as though early morning interruptions upset him. "What is it?"

"Looks like there's robbery goin' on here, Sam."

The man called Sam looked, and lowered his hand with the turner in it. His scowl deepened. "What the hell you fellers doin'?" he demanded gruffly.

"They're robbing me," Elihu Gorman repeated. "They came in with drawn guns, got me out of bed, and brought me out here 'n' took my money belt. Dammit, you can see what they've done, can't you?"

"I can see," Sam said, walking forward,

still holding his griddle-cake turner. "Gimme that belt," he ordered Tex. The belt sailed through the air. Sam caught it with his free hand, opened one of the pockets, and peered in. His eyes popped wide open. He dropped the turner and opened several other compartments of the belt. Each time his eyes reflected astonishment. He was still holding the belt when Tom said: "There's forty thousand dollars in that belt, mister. Every dollar of it was stolen from the Beatty bank by this man here. He was the town banker until night before last."

"Y'mean he cleaned out his own bank?"

"That's right."

"That is a lie!" stormed Elihu Gorman. "These men got me out of. . . ."

"Shut up," Sam snarled, looking from Tom to Tex and back to Gorman. "Joe, come up here." The man with the shotgun came warily forward. "Gimme that thing," Sam said, taking the shotgun. "Here, squat down there and count this money."

For a moment Gorman's frown reflected perplexity, then his face cleared and he opened his mouth to speak. The man called Sam waved the riot gun. "I said shut up, mister. I meant it. Every time someone interrupts, Joe's goin' to have to start all over again. He can't cipher so good."

"You count it then," Tom said.

Sam's disgruntled look deepened. "An' you keep quiet, too, mister. Besides, I can't cipher at all, an' that's worse'n what little Joe knows about it."

They stood there in the freshening daylight, watching the paunchy man squatting in the dust of the empty roadway counting money with knitted brows and moving lips. Somewhere behind the stage station someone was dragging chain harness with a musical sound. Someone else was forking hay, too, Tom knew, because several horses whinnied in unison and blew their noses. Finally the paunchy man folded the money back into the belt, stood up, and gazed at them all. "Heap of money in here, Sam," he said with awe in his voice.

"Well, dammit, how much money?"

"Forty thousand dollars."

Sam lowered the shotgun. "Mister," he said to Gorman, "where'd you get that money?"

Gorman had his answer ready. "I just sold a ranch," he said in a strong and convincing voice. "I'm going north to locate in Utah."

Sam's gaze studied Gorman through a silent moment, then his attention shifted to Tom. "You say he stole it?"

"I do. He was the banker at Beatty until

night before last. He stole the money and. . . ."

"Are you the law in Beatty, mister?"

"No, the law's Sheriff Tim Pollard."

Sam nodded. "That's right. I know Pollard. How come he ain't with you?"

"He's out with another posse."

Sam took the money belt from Joe, handed over the shotgun, and turned his back on them, walking toward the stage station. "Fetch 'em along," he growled at Joe. "Breakfast time."

They entered the station and met the startled look of three freshly washed male passengers who were just sitting down at the plank table. Sam was busy at a wood stove in one corner of the room. Those vertical lines between his eyes had not disappeared; he was deep in thought. Elihu Gorman protested loudly at being forced to eat at the same table with the outlaws who had just tried to steal his money. Sam, stacking griddle cakes on a thick crockery platter, started for the table. "Mister," he said dourly, "even outlaws got to eat. Why don't you just shut up and fill your gut?" Gorman subsided.

The three strangers at the table ate furtively, from time to time eyeing Joe, who remained by the door, his shotgun covering them all. They were nearly through breakfast when he sang out: "Northbound's comin'. You fellers got ten minutes 'fore fresh horses are hitched to the southbound."

One of the bystanders at the table raised his head. "I'm goin' north, not south, dammit."

Sam, seating himself at the table, looked up. "Be half hour before the northbound's ready to pull out. Driver's got to eat an' horses got to be changed. Southbound's already hitched up." He looked at his plate. "Half hour ain't long, pardner. Have a smoke and relax."

They all heard the southbound stage rocket up amid a rattle of loose tugs and shod hoofs, and brake to a long halt. Sam continued to eat imperturbably but Joe fidgeted at the door. Voices rose and the scent of dust rode the still air. A burly, whiskered man burst past the door, saw Joe, and stopped stockstill, mouth open but wordless. He was a leathery-visaged man of indeterminate years with bright blue eyes. "What the hell," he breathed finally. "Joe! What you doin'?"

"Been an attempted robbery here," Sam said dryly without looking up from his plate. "The dude here says these two with their hats on robbed him."

The driver circled the table so as not to get between the shotgun and the table, and said: "I'll be damned. Ain't it kind o' early in the day for that kind of stuff?"

"Your griddle cakes are in the oven," Sam said, chewing thoughtfully. "Coffee's in the pot."

The driver removed his hat, shoved gloves into it, and put the hat upon the table. He looked at the seated men a moment, then headed for the stove. Sam said: "No passengers, George?"

From the oven the driver mumbled a negative answer before heading for the table with a plate in his hands. "Joe," he said, looking backward, "be a mite careful with that thing, will you?"

From the doorway Joe smiled.

Tom stood up. Tex cast a swift glance at Joe, and, seeing no movement, also arose. Farther down the table the stationmaster sighed, pushed back his plate, drained off the last of his coffee, and pushed himself upright. "You ready to roll?" he asked Elihu Gorman.

"But I'm going north," the banker protested.

"You're goin' south," Sam said firmly. "Hell, ridin' stages this time of day is right pleasant, mister. You shouldn't mind a little delay."

"I just came from the south. I'm Utah bound, I told. . . ."

"Mister," Sam cut in, "there's just one way to find out who is a liar here, and that's to send the herd of you back to Beatty. Folks down there'll know who's a thief and who ain't. Now get up an' let's be movin'. Can't hold the stage up. Hard enough keepin' to schedules as it is."

Gorman marshaled arguments but they fell on stony ground. The stationmaster took the shotgun and drove Tom, Tex, and Gorman out to the waiting coach. There, he put the shotgun aside, sucked his teeth a moment, and said: "Mister, you said you was a rancher?"

"That's right. I sold out down south and I'm going. . . ."

"Yeah, I recollect all that." Sam regarded Elihu with an unblinking stare. "Joe, go fetch them guns over there in the road." When the guns were brought forward, Sam took them both, hefted them, and frowned. "You boys ready to go back?" he asked Tom and Tex.

Tom nodded. "We are. Give the guns to the driver. He can hand them over to Sheriff Pollard at Beatty."

Sam shook his head. "Naw. Why bother the driver with 'em?" He held both guns out, butts forward. When Tom hesitated, he shoved the gun into his hand. "Go ahead, mister, take it."

Tex accepted his gun and holstered it, but Tom stared straight into the stationmaster's eyes. "Are you thinking there might be a reward on us?" he asked. "And maybe we might be worth more dead than alive?"

Sam's expression looked pained. "There's the shotgun, against that wheel yonder. I couldn't reach it before you threw down on me, pardner."

Tom still made no move to take the gun. "Why are you doing this?" he demanded.

The stationmaster bent forward from the waist, dropped the pistol into Tom's holster, then reached for one of Elihu Gorman's hands and held it out palm upward. "You ever seen a rancher with hands as soft and pink as these?" He dropped the hand and shoved the money belt into Tex's hand. "Ever see a rancher's face as white as his?" he asked. Tom slowly smiled and turned toward the coach. "Maybe you can't cipher," he told the stationmaster, "but you can sure read people."

XVI

Elihu Gorman rode in a sulky slouch until Beatty appeared far ahead on the down-grade, then he drew up on the seat, his face turning pale, and, although Tom, who was closely watching him, thought he was going to speak, he said nothing.

The sun was riding high overhead, lemon-yellow and blindingly bright. Beatty was drowsing; horses at hitch rails stood hip-shot, eyes drooping and lower lips hanging slackly. Except for a number of idle men sitting in the shade along the plank walks there was no movement as the stage drew down to a halt and Tom stepped out. Gorman was next to get down, and Tex came last. Across the road in front of the hotel a man called sharply to someone. At the livery barn Mike Grogan recognized Tom, and stared, rooted to the ground. Another man who recognized all three stage passengers scuttled into the bank.

Tom took Gorman's arm and started south toward the sheriff's office. Tex, walking behind them, was triumphantly smiling.

Deputy Havestraw was in but Tim Pollard was still out with a posse. Havestraw was embarrassed and uncertain until Judge Montgomery burst in with a following of curious townsmen. "Lock that man up!" the judge thundered, jutting his face toward Elihu. "He robbed the bank."

Havestraw moved, finally, putting Elihu in a cell and padlocking him there. Tex leaned against the wall making a cigarette and feeling good, even smiling into Montgomery's white, angry face.

Tom considered the judge's expression without speaking, then turned his back on him, crossed to an iron stove where a coffee pot sat, and filled a tin cup. He drank with his back to the room.

Judge Montgomery was uncomfortable. He had something to say but Tom's back made it hard to speak. Eventually he turned on his heel and left the office.

There was a buzz of voices in the room. When Tom had emptied the cup, he faced around. Jack Havestraw had the money belt and was counting the bills on Tim Pollard's desk; he did it reverently, and, when he finished, he looked up into the still faces clustered around the desk. "Forty thousand dollars," he breathed softly. "Exactly what was stolen."

Tom caught Tex's eye and started for the door. Tex followed him out into the shimmering heat and across the road to the Royal Antler Saloon. Roy the bartender's impassivity slipped; his mouth dropped open.

"You fellers back?" he asked pointlessly.

"Sour mash," Tom said. "Two of 'em."

"Sheriff's lookin' for you," Roy confided, squinting around the nearly empty room.

Tex beamed a big smile. "Yeah, we just come from his jailhouse."

"Old Montgomery's bayin' at the moon for your hides, too."

Tom drank and nodded for a refill. "Hot out," he said. Roy filled both glasses the second time, leaned on the bar, and studied the two sun-darkened faces. "What the hell's goin' on around here, anyway?" he asked plaintively.

"We just brought the bank robber back," Tex said. "Elihu Gorman. He's locked up at Pollard's jail."

"No." Roy was dumbfounded. "Elihu Gorman?"

Tom twisted from the waist and gazed around the room. There were a dozen men lounging at the tables. Four of them were engaged in a desultory poker game. Hurrying boot steps thudded along the plank walk beyond the doors and a man entered. He stopped, squinting into the shaded room, then headed for the bar with a broad grin. It was Gerald Finnerty. "Hey!" he said, putting both hands on the counter and leaning toward Tom. "I just heard. You two been pretty busy."

Tom nodded to Roy for a third drink. Finnerty reached for the glass as he spoke. "Montgomery was just tellin' me." The drink went down; Finnerty blew out a breath and his eyes watered slightly. "He was pleased as punch, didn't even haggle over the hay price like he used to do."

Tom gradually drew up against the bar. "The hay price?"

"Sure, for that twenty tons I had the boys bring in for him."

Tex choked on his third drink and dabbed at his eyes. Roy solicitously got him a glass of water. "Trail dust'll do that to a feller," Roy murmured. "Drink this here water."

"Finnerty, did you sell the judge twenty tons of hay?"

The rancher's smile dwindled; the light died slowly in his eyes. "Sure. You sent word it'd be all right, Tom."

"I did? Who told you that?"

"Miss Antoinette."

Everyone's attention was briefly diverted by a cry of joy from the doorway to the card room. It was Miss Eloise who had just caught sight of Tex and was rushing toward him, arms outflung.

Tom took Finnerty's arm and guided him farther along the bar. "Miss Antoinette told you I'd said it was all right to sell her paw twenty tons of hay?" he asked.

"She sure did, Tom. The afternoon everyone was out lookin' for you 'n' Tex."

Tom let go of the cowman's arm. He called for Roy to bring two more drinks, downed his in one gulp, and headed for the door. Behind him, Tex was seeking unsuccessfully to break out of the iron embrace of Miss Eloise.

The bank was nearly empty when Tom entered it. A smiling clerk informed him that the judge had gone home for his midday meal and would not return probably until late in the afternoon. As Tom listened, he detected the sound of slow-riding horsemen coming into Beatty from the north. He went outside and watched as Sheriff Pollard and five dust-encrusted horsemen plodded through the hot sunlight. When Tim saw Tom standing in front of the bank, he drew up, staring. Finally he dismounted, flung his reins to one of the posse men, and walked stiffly forward into the shade of the overhang. His mustache was limply drooping and his shoulders sagged. "Hotter'n the hubs of hell," he said tiredly. "Well, what're you doin' back here?"

"Brought Gorman and the money back."

Pollard turned this over in his mind. "Gorman, eh? I ain't surprised. Just the same I wished you'd've let me know."

"You wouldn't have believed it."

Pollard's forehead wrinkled. "I think I would have," he replied. "Where is he now?"

"In your lock-up with Havestraw."

"I see, and you look like a bomb goin' somewhere to explode. What's the matter now?"

"Montgomery."

"Over hay?" Pollard asked shrewdly.

"Yes. He got twenty tons under false pretences."

Pollard's eyes crinkled nearly closed. He studied Tom's angry face for a moment before speaking. "Now look-a-here, Tom, you're workin' mighty hard at makin' a mountain out of a molehill."

"I didn't say he could have that hay."

"All right. You didn't say he could have it. Before you go stirrin' up trouble, you 'n' the judge better set down and powwow. I've known him a heap longer'n you have and Phil Montgomery don't pull underhanded stuff. If he got that hay, he thought he was gettin' it legally."

"Like he jumped to the conclusion I robbed his bank?"

"That wasn't no conclusion, boy. He showed me a note you'd signed."

Tom rocked up on the balls of his feet. "You've been out of town quite a while, haven't you? Better go ask Gorman who wrote that note . . . and who forged my name to it."

"I will, Tom, I will. But meantime, you hang an' rattle until I get some time an' I'll look into this hay-stealin' business."

The sheriff removed his hat, mopped his forehead, and replaced the hat. Down the roadway, in front of his office, men were moving among their tired horses. He groaned. "They'll be wantin' their posse pay. I'd better go. Remember what I said, Tom. Set tight for a while."

Tom went to his room at the hotel, called for the water boy, and soaked in a blissfully cool bath for nearly an hour. When he reëntered the room for fresh clothing, he found Tex sitting there, feet cocked on the sill, gazing out the window. He spoke a short greeting and began to dress.

"Finnerty had your money with him," Tex said, without looking around.

"I'll see him."

"About that hay, Tom."

"No lectures, Tex. I just got one from Pollard."

"This ain't no lecture. I told Miss Toni it was all right for her to have Finnerty fetch it to the barn."

"You what?"

Tex still did not look around. His hat was pushed back and his pale eyes roamed the far distance. "Just before I left her and Eloise at the creek, I told her it was all right."

Tom went to the dresser and began combing his hair. His face was red with smoldering wrath. "Why, Tex? You knew I didn't want him to have that hay."

"Well, like I told her, I figured I could soften you up before we got back."

Tom put the comb down and leaned upon the dresser, gazing at himself in the mirror. He finally finished dressing and started for the door. Without seeing him, Tex knew he was leaving. "Where you going now?" His voice asked from the window.

"To see Montgomery."

"Whoa," Tex said, dropping his feet and standing up. "Before you do that, let's say our good byes."

Tom had the doorknob in his fist. He said nothing until Tex turned to face him. He searched Earle's face, saw the resolution there, and lowered his brows. "Over twenty tons of hay, Tex?"

"You know better'n that, Tom. I told you I was leaving when we got Gorman."

"But you didn't leave."

Tex shrugged. "Figured I'd see he got delivered is all."

"If I forget about the damned hay?"

Tex shook his head. "I just told you, Tom, it ain't the damned hay. I told you a month back it was you. It still is." Tex started to cross the room slowly. "Anyway, they'll be working the cattle in the high country pretty quick now and there'll be lots of work."

Tom hadn't believed this argument when Tex had used it before. He knew his partner too well, had heard him curse the thin, cold air of the high country too many times. He leaned upon the door. "Wait a week and I'll go with you, Tex."

Earle stopped, his eyes lighting up. "You don't mean that, do you?"

Tom meant it. He had done much thinking of late, particularly on the ride back with Gorman his prisoner. Although he had triumphed in some ways in his feud with the town, none of the victories had been as he had planned, nor had they left him feeling proud. In fact, he felt somewhat ashamed of himself. He hadn't, of course, been directly responsible for Moses Beach's stroke, but he suspected that he had contributed to it. He hadn't forced Gorman to rob the bank, either, but he had certainly helped to drive him to it. He hadn't yet broken the judge, but he had made Tex do something shameful in his effort to hurt Montgomery, and perhaps that was even worse than making the judge kneel.

There were, he had thought on the drive back with Gorman, some undertakings that you simply could not make appear decent — like a stand-up fight — no matter how hard you tried. It had been a slow-arriving and bitter realization, and yet the proof was all around him. At this very moment it was in Tex Earle's face, in his poorly concealed disapproval, in his pale, boyish eyes, and finally it was in Tex's wish to leave Beatty and its memories behind.

"Yeah, I mean it, Tex. We'll leave. . . ."

They descended the stairs side-by-side and went out into the lengthening afternoon bound for the Royal Antler. There, they had a solemn drink together, then Tex went in search of Eloise to tell her the news. There, too, Gerald Finnerty came upon Tom again and gravely placed a big roll of soiled bills on the bar top; around the money was a limp strand of buckskin holding it together.

"Count it," Finnerty said. "It's all there. You got my note on you?"

"Montgomery's got it at the bank. I'll get it for you."

"No hurry," the cowman said, beckoning to the barman. "Tom, you ever think about settlin' down around here?"

Tom accepted the drink, inclined his head toward Finnerty, and downed it. "No," he said with a shade more emphasis than was necessary.

"Well, you know I got that option on the place adjoinin' me, and it's a real fine parcel of land. It'll run easy five thousand head year around."

"You need that for expansion," Tom said, turning his empty glass in its own little puddle of dampness. "Besides, I. . . ."

"Naw, I don't want to expand. What I want is a good neighbor there who'll run cattle with me. You know, sort of work roundups with me."

Tom was going to speak when a man's voice raised in surprise and anger interrupted him. He and Finnerty turned in time to see Tex's hat sail across the room as though possessed of wings. Beyond Earle's tall back Miss Eloise was aiming another blow. "Run out on me, will you?" she screeched at the swiftly ducking Texan. "Sweet talk me, then run out as soon as . . . !"

"I'll go get your note," Tom said to Finnerty with a quick, hard smile, and hastened out of the saloon.

XVII

He walked through the lengthening shadows toward the bank. A low breeze was freshening the air and people were again abroad now that the day's heat was mostly past. He saw Deputy Havestraw talking to a cowboy in front of Moses Beach's store and, through the weaving press of pedestrians, caught a glimpse of Toni Montgomery. He left the plank walk, stepped out into the roadway, and heat rose up around him from the dust.

At the bank a clerk led him to Elihu Gorman's office. There, Judge Montgomery with spectacles pushed up onto his forehead was gazing at a stack of papers on the desk. The judge glanced up and nodded. Tom returned the nod, waited until the clerk was gone, and spoke. "I want the note Gorman forged my name to," he said.

Without a word Judge Montgomery held up a paper. Tom took it, folded it, and stuffed it into a pocket. "About that hay," he said. "It was brought to you by mistake."

"Mistake?" the judge said, puzzled. "What mistake, Mister Barker?"

"Your daughter and a friend of mine misunderstood me when I said you were to have no hay."

"Are you inferring that my daughter is a liar, Mister Barker?"

"You heard what I said, Judge. I didn't call anyone a liar. I said you got that hay by mistake."

Judge Montgomery continued to gaze at Tom even after an uncomfortable silence settled between them. Then he got slowly to his feet. "Doesn't it appear a little ridiculous to you, Mister Barker, to carry a grudge for nearly fifteen years?" He made a deprecatory gesture. "After all, I didn't willingly hurt you."

Tom said dryly: "You've seen horses with broken legs get shot, haven't you?"

"Certainly."

"I doubt if a horse ever breaks his leg on purpose, Judge."

"That's ridiculous, Barker."

"Almost as ridiculous as turning a little kid over to his father when you knew damned well he'd get a beating."

"I didn't know," Judge Montgomery said, coloring. "I had no idea at all."

Tom looked coldly down into the red face. "Then, why didn't you ask Sheriff Pollard," he demanded, "when you took that little kid to the sheriff's office?" He stopped at the door, opened it, and said: "You can either pay me fifty dollars a ton for that damned hay, or you can return it."

"Fifty dollars! Hell, Barker. . . ."

"I know. You'll see me in hell first."

Tom returned to the street, read the note Gorman had forged, tore it into tiny pieces, and consigned it to the gently rustling wind.

"There's an ordinance against clutterin' the roadways," Sheriff Pollard said, coming up and stopping. "You been to see the judge?"

"Yes."

"He reward you for fetchin' back Gorman?"

"No."

"Hmmmm. That's odd. Oh, well, it don't matter to a man of your means, does it?" Pollard waved at a group of riders swinging past, sun-bronzed, lean men riding horses that all carried one iron. "Just run Clint Ingersoll and some of his freighter friends back to their camp. Drunk," the sheriff said with mild disgust. "Drunk in the middle of the day." He caught Tom's glance and held it. "Clint said they were goin' to pull out tomorrow, heading for Mirage and points north."

Tom understood what Tim Pollard was

telling him. He was grateful for the way the sheriff was doing it. He looked across the road, where sunset was splashing a dozen shades of red over wooden false fronts. "Things'll settle down then," he said, remembering suddenly that he'd forgotten to get Finnerty's note from the judge.

Pollard smiled. "If they get too quiet, I'll get lazy."

"Buy you a drink," Tom said, facing straight ahead.

The sheriff started past. "Maybe later, Tom. I never drink before supper."

Tom watched him move on, then crossed toward the Queens & Aces Café. He was almost to the door when Toni Montgomery stopped him. He touched his hat.

"Tom, can you spare me a few minutes?"

"I can always spare you a few minutes, Toni. You know that without asking."

"Then walk with me."

They went south along the plank walk until the boards ran out, and they continued along through the day's late and softening shadows that faded at last into the merging sky, until Toni stopped and swung to face him.

"You're leaving Beatty, aren't you, Tom?"

For a second he was surprised, then he said: "Eloise told you, didn't she?"

"Yes. Did you know that she is in love with Tex?"

It was on the tip of his tongue to say he didn't know saloon girls loved. Instead though, he looked beyond her hair to the changing lights of the far horizon and shrugged. "She could do much worse, Toni."

"She has already done worse. That's what she told me a few hours ago. She's been married before."

His eyes returned to her face, then fled outward again. Stark and naked in the lowering evening stood a gnarled tree. He remembered it from his youth — Beatty's hang tree. More than one horse thief and outlaw had writhed his last precious moments from its limbs. "You picked a hell of a place to stop," he said suddenly, and took her hand guiding her along through the twilight toward town. "The judge'll be waiting for his supper."

She went willingly for only a hundred yards, then stopped and drew away from him. "Why are you going, Tom?"

"I think you know," he answered.

"But I'd rather have you tell me."

"Why? So you can crow?"

Her head moved slightly from side to side. "You know me better than that."

He drew in a big breath. "No one likes to

be wrong, Toni. Maybe I like it least of all, because I've wasted a lot of years waiting to come down here and be top lash."

"Is going back where you came from going to be any better?"

He looked into her gray, wide, and liquid eyes. "I don't believe I like having you look inside me, Toni. Anyway, you might see something you don't want to see."

"What is it, Tom? What's back there where you came from? A girl?"

He smiled. "No girl, Toni, just a lot of big mountains with snow the year around, high meadows, and ice-cold creeks. Pines and fir trees and open range. Just more cattle country."

She was silently gazing at the crooked rim of the northeastern skyline, nearly obscured now by darkness, lost in the depths of her thoughts. "Tex told Eloise about the hay," she said gently.

Anger stirred in him. "Damn that hay anyway," he cursed. "He can have it . . . have all of it as far as I'm concerned."

She watched his face twist, then smooth out again when he caught her watching him.

"You tell him that for me," he growled.

"Tom? Don't you realize he could have it anyway? You haven't kept track of time. Your options expired while you were chasing

Elihu Gorman."

This sobered him. He began to trace back the spun-out summer days in his memory. Then he squinted down at her. "Why didn't he say that today, when I was in the bank?"

"Probably for the same reason Sheriff Pollard hasn't told you that Clint Ingersoll killed your father while you and Tex were gone. They don't want to add to your troubles."

He stared at her. "Ingersoll killed him?"

"Yes, Tom."

He was surprised that all he felt was mild astonishment. There was no sense of loss, no sense of pain or remorse, no desire for vengeance. "How, Toni?"

"Several men were drinking out at the freighter's camp. No one knows exactly how it happened, just that it was a gunfight and that your father was killed."

She touched his arm, looking up into his eyes. He was looking blankly past her, waiting patiently for the swiftly flowing childhood scenes to pass. Then his expression altered; he looked at her hand, felt its pressure, and was warmed by its message. Whatever was there in the night lay in both of them. He put up his other hand, covered her fingers, and continued on more slowly toward the orange-yellow lights of Beatty.

"Did you ever hear the story of my mother, Toni?"

Her reply was simple and grave. "Yes, once, a number of years back, I eavesdropped when Sheriff Pollard and the judge were talking on the porch. I afterward cried myself to sleep."

He remembered something with a start, something that appeared quite suddenly out of his memory and that, until that moment, he had not recollected at all. A little glass on the grave beside the headstone with withered forget-me-nots in it. He strode along, holding her hand and saying nothing.

Antoinette looked sideways at his profile in the pale night. There was a reserve about him, a hardness that was not altogether the product of bitter environment; for a space of seconds she was afraid of him. Then she recalled the way other men looked upon him and thought how illuminating one man's judgment of another man was. Women were not good judges of men; they saw only what was pleasing to look upon, only what was handsome or smiling or laughing — or gentle. Men did not see these virtues, or, seeing them, did not include them in their weighing and measuring. Her father and Tim Pollard, for example, had reason to dislike Tom Barker — and yet neither of them really did dislike him. And Gerald Finnerty, and Roy the bartender, who had judged so many men, and Tex Earle. Even, she thought, Clint Ingersoll, who wanted to kill him — even him. He respected Tom or he would have shot him down before this, perhaps from hiding as most men killed other men on the frontier. His voice scattered her thoughts.

"I reckon a man can live down mistakes, can't he?"

"Of course he can, Tom."

"You know, I've taken more baths since I've been back here than I ever took before."

She looked up, not understanding until he went on.

"I keep feeling dirty, Toni. And it won't wash off."

A shadow rushed over her face, or seemed to, but she very wisely held her tongue.

They came to the edge of the plank walk, stepped up onto it, and progressed slowly northward. Across the roadway Sheriff Tim Pollard, sitting on a bench in front of his office, leaned a little, the better to identify them. Then he rocked back and ran a thoughtful hand under his mustache.

There was the thinnest of sickle moons. Patches of lamplight made squares of diluted light along the walk and out into the road. Horsemen jogged past, trailing fragments of pleasant conversation. When they passed the Royal Antler, Gerald Finnerty doffed his hat at Antoinette and threw Tom a solemn wink. Farther along, near Beach's emporium, Jack Havestraw stood in the shadows, sighing; he scarcely saw Tom at all.

As they neared the Montgomery home, he said: "Toni, if I got a buggy from the livery barn . . . would you go for a drive with me . . . later on?"

Her eyes held a glowing deepness, a sudden sweetness that made her face even prettier. Her lips, soft and pliable, moved — red and full and kindly. "I'd love to, Tom," she murmured. He noticed quite suddenly that her hair seemed almost auburn in the night, that her skin was flawlessly smooth. He heard himself speaking and recognized only the voice, not the words. "Eight o'clock?"

She squeezed his arm and left.

He thought of the Royal Antler but there was no urge. Instead, he crossed the road, went to the livery barn, and made the arrangements, and for a moment he had trouble remembering the now smiling hulk of a hostler. Then it all came back and he handed the man a coin. "I reckon I've been reprieved," he said.

The man laughed. "The loft's full of hay," he said by way of answer. Then, as Tom was walking away, the night hawk added: "Your horse and that other feller's horse come back from Red Stone stage station today. I got 'em stalled for you."

Tom went back out into the night. He felt good, as though a heavy weight had fallen away from him, as though something had gushed out of a fester deep inside him. He could hear and understand the soft laughter that came along the roadway on the night air, each rising and falling note of it. A lanky silhouette came toward him, angling across the road and scuffing up grouts of dust with each step. "Where you bound?" he asked as Tex stopped and peered through the darkness at him.

"Oh, it's you. Well, y'see, Eloise got plumb roiled at me this evening and I figure to take her riding in the moonlight and sort of. . . ."

"What moonlight?"

Tex cocked his head skyward, then looked down again. "In the cool of the evening then," he continued. "That way I figure she'll get over her notion of throwing things at me." A sudden thought struck Tex. "Y'know, for a female she's pretty good at aiming where she throws, too." He passed on into the barn, and Tom's attention was caught by four stalwart, striding men, moving noiselessly through the night toward the Royal Antler, their flat-heeled boots striking soundlessly against the earth beside the plank walk. Freighters. He searched out the tallest silhouette but could not recognize it in the gloom. It didn't matter, though; in a little while he would be driving out with Toni. There would be no meeting this night.

Tex came up beside him and halted, looking across the road at moving shadows. "Night hawk says you already got that top buggy with the yellow running gear."

"That's right."

"*Hmmmmm.* Driving out with no moon, Tom?"

A chuckle passed the big, dark man's lips as Tex stepped down into the roadway and trudged toward the Royal Antler. It was good when your partner kidded you because it only happened when he had no reservations in his mind about you.

XVIII

They drove through a pleasant night, breathing deeply of an atmosphere made fragrant by the scent of a sighing, cooling earth. The mare between her shafts plodded placidly with head hung and the yellow spokes threw back gyrating reflections of the thin moon. Beside him Antoinette murmured: "Tom, did you know it is possible to wait for something indefinitely without being conscious you were waiting at all?"

He leaned back with the lines slack in his hand. "Yes, I knew, Toni."

His jaw, she noticed, balanced his face. He had removed his hat and shafts of murky light touched his hair, making it darker, wavier; where it grew low upon his temples, it was pressed close. She had, in weeks past, made many private excuses for him, and it had been cruel the way things had worked out to rebuff them. It had not been an easy thing to take his part against the judge, nor had she done it openly, which was perhaps why the torment had been so scalding within her. But now, this night, it seemed to her that vindication had come. She had sensed it earlier when they had walked together through the twilight arm in arm, and the knowledge that her faith in him had not, after all, been misplaced was good knowledge. "When are you and Tex leaving, Tom?"

His head came up slightly as though he had seen something ahead of them. "We talked about pulling out in a week," he replied detachedly, as though speaking of two other men.

It was this tone that gave her a quick lift of the heart. She said no more. On both sides of them the land stretched off into a gradual merging lift and rise toward the distant hills. She recognized their direction, and, when the mesmerizing *clop-clop-clop* of the mare's hoofs had relaxed them both, she asked: "Where are we going?"

"Up by the creek," he answered. "Unless you'd rather go somewhere else."

"No," said Toni. "I was hoping you'd drive up there."

The mare was breathing deeply by the time Tom drew up and got down to loosen her check rein and tie her to a big willow. Somewhere behind him Toni could hear water tumbling over stones. He helped her down and led her to the base of an ancient cottonwood. She settled upon the ground, pulling him beside her. She laced her fingers together around drawn up knees, gazing at the high sky and its shimmering star fire. Silence settled around them in a soft, full wave.

Tom plucked a blade of dead grass, peeled it thoughtfully, and chewed it. He lay back loosely, legs thrust out, his body turning softly against the ground. He was, she thought, as thoroughly relaxed as a man could be; it was good to see him that way because she knew he hadn't often relaxed since returning to Beatty.

"This is mighty pleasant," he said around the drooping grass stem. "Damned pleasant."

It was her presence, she knew, that did this to him, but she was not a vain woman. Any woman's presence would have brought out this relaxed mood; he was a man with deep hungers, with strong emotions, a solid man, physically alive and strong. He had his desires, his thoughts, and his memories. Her gaze clouded over. It was the memories she would have to combat. "Don't go to sleep," she murmured, and he laughed up at her.

"I won't."

"Tom what does tomorrow hold?"

He kept his eyes on her face, her throat where the strong pulse was beating, and said: "Whatever you want it to hold. Tomorrow never comes, Toni, it's here. It's really today and it holds what you've made it yield."

This was a side of him she had not seen before. Their eyes met and held, then she looked skyward. He was also a deep man; one with private thoughts. "Tom?"

"Yes."

"I wish you had come back differently."

"You mean changed?"

"No. I wish you'd come back for a different reason."

He looked away from her, let his gaze wander along the base of the rising bald hills, and was silent for a while. Then he murmured: "I'll go away differently." And she heard the long sweep of an indrawn breath in his chest. "It's a strange life, Toni. You're driven to do things that you don't really understand until you're well into them . . . then they don't look as good as you'd thought they would."

"Isn't it better to see them in the right light, than not to see them that way, ever?"

"I reckon," he conceded. "Only it doesn't take away the shame."

"You've done nothing here to be really ashamed of."

"You don't know, Toni."

"I think I do. I've kept my eyes open."

He looked again at her, this time with a dry little smile. "And your ears as well?"

"Yes. Only I've never put any faith in gossip, Tom. Especially around Beatty. When there's not much else for folks to do, they talk about other folks."

His smile lingered. For a while neither of them spoke, then she asked about Tex.

"Tex? Oh, I've known him since a year or two after I left Beatty. We pardnered up and traveled from summer range to winter range and back again."

"No, I didn't mean his background. I meant . . . is he going away with you?"

"Yes."

"What about Eloise?"

How did you tell a girl like Antoinette that men, especially drifters like Tex Earle, took — they did not give? "I expect she'll forget him, Toni." It sounded resolved to him, the way he'd said it, until he caught her staring down at him, then it sounded callous. He threw the grass stem away. "Well, a man doesn't marry every woman he sparks. It's a sort of companionship thing, y'see."

"With us, too, Tom?"

"No, because that's different. We were kids together." His face softened. "You know, Toni, lots of nights I've lain in my soogans, remembering things we did. Climbing into the bell tower that time, and putting that skunk in Miz Grogan's geranium patch." His dark gaze brightened with reflection. "You didn't seem like a girl in those days. I didn't think of you as one." He cocked his head at her. "Did you know that?"

She smiled a trifle ruefully. "Sometimes it was pretty hard being your kind of a tomboy," she said, remembering, too, how she had mooned around the house when they were not together and recalling each little stab of pain he had brought to her heart when his words grew spiteful or scornful.

"Naw, you were always a tomboy, Toni."

She was silently hugging her knees and looking straight ahead. "That was so long ago, Tom."

"Not really."

"Could we ever go back?"

He looked at her profile. "No. I reckon you're right. It was a long time ago, at that." He was seeing her differently, the swelling fullness of her blouse, and her thigh where the skirt was drawn tightly around it. No, she wasn't the same person at all. He stirred and she spoke swiftly, fearful that he was becoming restless.

"Tim Pollard likes you, Tom."

He plucked another blade of grass. His feelings here were mixed. It was impossible not to like the sheriff, and it was impossible not to respect him, which of course meant much more. "He's a good man, Toni. I have nothing against him."

"But when you first came back you did."

"Yes. But I told you . . . that's all past now."

"Don't you want to be top lash any more?"

He bit down on the grass stem. "Who told you I wanted to be that?"

"No one had to tell me, Tom. You've changed a lot since we were kids, but basically you haven't changed. I just thought you had. Well . . .?"

"No, I don't care about that any longer. It's part of something I'd like to forget."

She spoke in the gentlest, softest voice, looking fully down at him. "And the judge?"

"Him, too. Like I said, I want to forget all that."

"But you don't like the judge, Tom."

He had no ready answer because he actually did not like her father, had never liked him in fact, but as a youth the dislike had simply been because he was her father and used to bawl her out when they stayed away from home too long or were caught in some mischievous act. "I can forget that," he mumbled, and straightened up off the ground. "And he can have the damned hay."

"You'll lose money on those options."

"Not much. Anyway, the interest Finnerty paid me will make it up and then some."

He sat with his elbows on his knees, his head thrust forward, and his dark profile blending with the shadows. His lip corners had a tough set to them. Toni gazed at him with an interest that came only of deep personal interest. "I wish you weren't leaving," she said quietly. "I wish you'd stay, Tom."

He made no move but his jaw muscles rippled, his gaze gentled, and after a moment longer of hard concentration he turned to face her. There were no words on his lips. It was a difficult moment; the night around him was full of confused and confusing emotions. He changed expression, was on the verge of smiling at her. She did not smile back. Earnestness held her face dark and still. She put forth her hand; he took it. Her fingers closed around his palm suddenly strong, holding to him, pressing some of her thoughts into him. Abruptly she sought to draw her hand away, but he held her, drew her off balance toward him. But she braced against the pressure and freed her hand, jumping to her feet. "Maybe we'd better go back," she said in an unsteady, low voice.

The quick, sad call of a coyote broke upon the stillness. He got up more slowly and turned to swipe at the seat of his trousers. He felt uncomfortable and within him somewhere there stabbed a shaft of pain.

He went without another word to the buggy mare, untied her, left the check rein loose, and handed Toni up onto the seat, got in beside her, and flipped the lines. The mare turned instinctively and started the long trip back. After a mile of hush and discomfort he said: "Why do things have to happen like they do? It was so damned pleasant up there with you."

Her reply was warm and apologetic. "I'm sorry, Tom. I really am. It was my fault." She took his free hand in both hers and held it with her fingers curled tightly around it. "It was me. It was something I felt back there."

"But Toni, if I didn't go away . . . what then?"

She looked at him. "What do you mean, what then?"

"Well, hell, the judge doesn't like me. Pollard, he's not so easy to figure out. He's been kind to me. . . ."

"He likes you. I know he does."

"Then he's the only one around who does."

"No, I do, Tom."

His hand in her lap twisted, caught at her fingers, and bruised them with unconscious feeling. "Thanks."

"Honestly, Tom, I think most people around Beatty like you." He shook his head at that. She drew up slightly on the seat and bent forward to emphasize her words. "The cowmen do, I know. They won't ever tell you so, Tom, but what you did for Gerald Finnerty is the kind of thing they judge a man by."

He understood this because he was also a man who judged other men by their actions. Still, he could not separate the bitterness that had driven him to return to Beatty with the hatred in his heart, from the things he had done since he had returned, and he was certain others saw in him, and in his actions, only the coldness, the hunger for vengeance that had governed everything he had done.

Toni's next words cut across his thoughts, driving them out. "Give Beatty a second chance, Tom. I can't explain away how you were treated years back. But I can tell you this. Not even the judge wishes you ill now."

He thought of his boyhood, of his days with Toni, of the fine days full of promise and golden sunlight, days that no other part of the land had ever successfully duplicated for him. And he thought of the soft, mellowed stone in the cemetery. He longed to belong, to forget what had happened twelve years earlier, and what had happened since he had returned. He longed only to put down roots and. . . .

"Stop the buggy, Tom."

He obeyed. She was looking fully at him and her face was white, her eyes enormous, her lips slightly parted as though she had made some desperate decision. When next she spoke, the words were squeezed out, unreal sounding.

"Kiss me."

He drew her to him and found her mouth. A soft, stifled sob came from her throat; her breath beat savagely upon his cheek, and her hands felt for him, drew him even closer.

It was as though something exploded inside his skull. He bruised her with his strength and let the wild full run of his temper, the force of his will go free. It came out and broke over her, suddenly, this fierce hot longing that he had not known until this moment was within him for her, and it passed over them both. Deep down there in the hollow of the land, Beatty lay, a dark mass of irregularity in the warm blackness, touched less by moonlight than by its own squares of soft orange. All around was a loneliness, while circling the valley, chunked up heavily against the sky, were the bald hills.

XIX

He stepped to the bar with a pleasant tiredness in him, had his drink, took glass and bottle to the wall table, and dropped down. Roy the bartender kept looking at him. Tom Barker's face was a brooding mask, normally, but now Roy saw in it a kind of odd and unnatural beauty. This look fascinated Roy; it was not a thing men saw often in the faces of other men.

"Hey, Roy, you seen that Barker feller in here tonight?"

Roy looked around. "Right over there," he said matter-of-factly. "As plain as the nose on your face."

The cowboy crossed to Tom's side and stopped. "Mister," he said. "You got a pardner called Tex?"

Tom blinked out of his reverie. "I have. What about him?"

" 'Pears he bit a chunk off he can't chew."

"A fight," Tom said swiftly, arising. "Where?"

"Out back o' the livery barn."

He asked no more and the cowboy rushed out of the saloon in his wake. It was beyond midnight now, with very little showing of Beatty in the darkness. There were a number of horses standing idly at the livery barn's outside rail and near them, blissfully asleep, lay a drunken drifter, head cradled in his arms.

He rushed the full-lighted distance of the barn's long main aisle and out into the cooling gloom beyond where motionless shapes of men stood, faces savagely intent upon a sprawled silhouette moving feebly in the dust of the back lot. It was Tex; he was down and he was hurt. Even in that bad light Tom could see the dilation of his pupils, the flung-back smear of blood along his cheek, and the scrabbling, numb gropings of his fingers in the dirt. He would have gone forward but a thick arm stopped him. It was Grogan, the liveryman. He said softly: "Better let 'em finish it, Mister Barker. There's three more of them freighters out there."

Tom raked the shadows with a hard look in his eyes. There were perhaps ten men in the darkness, all motionless. Some were cattlemen; he recognized their faces. Several were townsmen and three of them were freighters, lips skinned back, smiling at the big, taut figure bending above the downed man: Clint Ingersoll, shorn of belt and gun and with cocked fists at the ready.

"Get up," Ingersoll was snarling. "Y'dirty mother's son. Get up!"

Tex rolled over, got to his knees, and

braced with both hands against the ground. He shook his head and bubbling sounds came from his throat.

"Put the boots to him," a freighter growled. "He ain't goin' to get up."

Ingersoll moved menacingly forward as though to comply and a soft, silken voice only slightly roughened by feeling said: "Keep it fair, Ingersoll. No boots."

Tom found the face; it was Gerald Finnerty. He had one hand resting lightly on his holstered gun. Around him were other cowmen, their faces closed down around a similar feeling for fairness.

Ingersoll drew up slightly, still holding his fists cocked. "Maybe you'd like some, too," he shot at the cowman.

Finnerty smiled very thinly. "Sure, put on your gun. I don't dog fight."

Ingersoll's gaze went back to Tex, who was getting clumsily to his feet. He waited only until Earle was staggering upright, then he went in. Fists crunched off bone and battered numb flesh, and Tex went down, rolled over, and lay breathing shallowly.

"He's out," a freighter crowed. "Dump some water on the whelp."

"He's had enough," an older man said, moving up into the reflected light of the barn. It was Tim Pollard. Tom stared in astonishment. "All right, it was a fair scrap. Now let's forget about it."

"The hell," Ingersoll said. "It's only just started."

"Dammit," Pollard snapped, "can't you see he's out?"

"Well, I ain't out, and I'm just gettin' warmed up."

Tom moved from behind Grogan's arm, stepped into the yellow glow facing Ingersoll. "I'd hate to see you go away unsatisfied," he said. "Anyway, I reckon your fight's more with me than with him."

Ingersoll turned heavily and glared. His lips parted. "Well, I'll be damned if it ain't top lash himself. Where you been hidin', Barker? We been all over town lookin' for you tonight."

There was a bloodshot brightness to the man's eyes and a flush of dark blood from throat to temple. Ingersoll had been drinking, yes, but more than that his blood was heated by the will to fight. Tom recognized this and a spasm of animal shock passed over him; it was an instantaneous flash that touched every nerve end, leaving him coldly calculating. An ancient, brutal eagerness flooded his mind. He knew what Ingersoll was going to do; it was as though they were thinking through one mind. The breath in his chest went deeper; his stomach pinched down, and the hard sloshing of his heart sounded loud in his own ears. His muscles turned loose and sweat ran under his clothing. Tim Pollard said in a high voice: "Hold it! You can't fight, Tom. Your lung ain't healed yet."

Then Ingersoll lunged for him, drove his big body forward, both fists flailing. Tom dug in his heels and shifted aside with a grunt. He grunted a second time as Ingersoll swept past and he threw a right fist at the freighter's ear, missed, and nearly lost his balance.

Ingersoll spun back and came on again. This time Tom settled himself and waited. But he missed again, and Ingersoll's momentum caught him, carried him back against the rough boards of the barn, and slammed him hard against wood. Through a roaring that did not altogether come from the bystanders he saw Ingersoll's big fists through a blur; he weaved away from them but caught one along the point of his jaw and his shoulders sagged; his arms partially dropped.

He turned away to take the beating along the side but each strike hurt him. It was like being struck with a pick handle; his ribs flashed pain into his skull and cleared that injured portion of his brain. He rolled along the wall, then dropped low, jammed his feet down hard, and shot forward, driving Ingersoll back, wrestling with him, their straining arms locked briefly, then he was clear to maneuver again, and he broke away, looping a hard blow to Ingersoll's chest that jarred the freighter and drove him off. They circled, weaving, ducking low, seeking openings. Ingersoll flung out a pawing hand and Tom knocked it aside. Ingersoll's next blow had the power of a lowered shoulder behind it. But Tom had seen him get set and moved farther out, leaving the freighter fanning air.

Next, the freighter feinted Tom closer and loosed a whipping uppercut. It grazed Tom's jaw raising an instantaneous red welt. But Ingersoll was off balance and still moving forward against his will. Tom's big arms fired twice, staggering the freighter with two hard strikes across the mouth. Ingersoll shuffled backward, great gulps of whistling breath gushing past torn lips, foamy and blood-flecked now. He circled, moving his shoulders and keeping his fists well forward, only slightly bent at the elbows. Someone was hanging a lantern near the barn's rear entrance; its light quickly found the fighters and made a pale circle around them. The bystanders were intently silent, mouths twisted and eyes glowing with battle lust. Blood dripped on Ingersoll's sweat-darkened shirt and Tom felt the throbbing cadenced beat of pain along the swelling side of his jaw.

Ingersoll leaped in close and swung. Tom met him with no inclination to move away. Big fists swung and meaty echoes mingled with grunts and torn snatches of hard breathing. Flesh and bone could not long stand this punishing exchange. Tom dropped flat onto his heels, head swimming and vision blurring. Then Ingersoll stumbled backward first, and the cowmen swore a fierce, common oath almost in unison. The freighters looked on, still and rock-faced.

They circled again and through battered lips Tom cursed Ingersoll in a bitter and steady undertone. "Fight," he said. "That's what you want to do, isn't it? Then quit backing up!"

Ingersoll jumped suddenly forward and struck Tom in the chest. Tom staggered. Ingersoll struck him again, and Gerald Finnerty grabbed Tim Pollard by the shirt front and shook him. *"Argh!"* he groaned, "he's going to open it up, damn him!"

Tom back-pedaled sluggishly, and Ingersoll rushed forward, sensing the kill, but he ran head-on into a massive blow that made his arms drop to his sides, made his mouth sag, and his eyes glaze over briefly. It had been a trick. He tried to get away. Barker's fist smashed him high across the bridge of the nose and claret spewed. The same fist, red and sticky, glanced across his cheek. Tom could feel the jolt of those solid blows all the way to his shoulder. It was like an electric shock. A faint mistiness swam before his eyes but he pinched them down nearly closed the better to see the twisting, graying face ahead. Then, in wildest desperation, Ingersoll rushed him with crooked fingers clawing for flesh or cloth. But he was too badly beaten; his co-ordination was numbed and Tom smashed him twice more across the face, bringing on a fresh spray of claret each time. Ingersoll suddenly stopped, planted his big legs wide apart, and stood there moving like a tree in a high wind. Tom struck him with all the strength remaining in him. Ingersoll absorbed the blow. Another blow, this one with a loud, sobbing grunt behind it, crashed into his face and Ingersoll's knees buckled; he bent slowly at the middle; his head dropped forward, and he fell full length into the weaving pattern of lantern light, pushing out to lie perfectly motionless. Into the deep stillness came his faint, broken breathing, a thinly bubbling sound.

Tom found someone facing him with a bucket of water. He plunged both bleeding hands into it, felt the sharp bite, and raised cupped hands to his face, dashed water into his eyes, and sucked back all the air he could get. Then he coughed and blood came, faintly pink, and he spat. Someone jostled him; he turned and gazed into the white and wide-eyed face of Tex; they attempted a grin at one another. "Guess I calculated wrong," Tex croaked. "The other time you done it, it looked so easy." Tex fingered his puffy face. "He caught you a couple of good ones, one there along the jaw. It's swelling up like a goose egg."

The freighters were helping Clint Ingersoll to his feet. They dumped water on him; he came out of it very groggily and slowly. Sheriff Pollard was talking aside to the cowmen. Someone handed Tom his belt gun and until he felt its coldness he did not know it had been knocked loose of its holster by the barn wall.

It was the night air as much as the water that revived him. His shirt was hanging in shreds and even the bandages across his chest were stained with blood and dirt. There was no sense of pain, really, but he ached in every muscle and joint.

"Hey, Barker," a gruff, angry-sullen voice called. "You got your gun . . . turn around here!"

Instantly Sheriff Pollard cried out. "Hold it! No gun play!"

The gruff voice snarled. "Who's goin' to stop it?"

Pollard's voice turned thinly dangerous. "Me! You fellers take Clint back to camp and get your wagons ready. I don't want to see a damned one of you around town come sunup."

Tom turned. The four freighters were glaring at Pollard. Each of them was armed and it was very clear that unless something stopped them they were going to precipitate a gunfight. "Wait!" Tom called. "Ingersoll . . . is that what you want?" The big freighter's eyes, nearly hidden in the swollen wreckage of his face, did not look straight at Tom, and Ingersoll said nothing. "Because if that's all you fellers'll settle for, I'll oblige you."

"Not alone you won't," Gerald Finnerty said succinctly. "Let 'em start it. I'd just as leave kill freighters tonight as not."

Pollard was protesting again but no one heeded him. Tom moved forward several steps, looking straight at Clint Ingersoll.

"Well?" he demanded.

Ingersoll drew himself up; he pushed clear of his companions and faced Tom. He held out both hands; they were swollen nearly twice their normal size. His meaning was instantly clear to everyone; he could neither draw nor fire a gun.

Tom looked at the other freighters. "You fellers trying to get him killed? He fought a good fight. Isn't that enough for you?"

One of the freighters shouldered past Ingersoll. He was a massive and squatty man with an overhanging, low brow and a bully's massive, thick jaw. "Not for me it ain't," he said. "Now I suppose you're goin' t'say you can't draw a gun, either?"

Tom did not seem to move at all but there was a flash and a roar and the freighter was spun half around. He staggered and cursed and ran a hand down his side. No one spoke. Clearly visible in the lamplight his hip holster was hanging, ripped apart from the shell belt, and his pistol lay thirty feet behind him in the moving light.

"Hell," a man breathed into the hush.

Finnerty and Tim Pollard recovered first. "Anyone else?" The rancher asked, and Pollard said: "Move! Go on now, go back to your camp and get ready to hitch up! Beatty's closed to freighters from now. Pass that along the freight roads, too. No more freighters welcome in Beatty."

Men shuffled off into the night. Tim Pollard waited until they were all gone, then he went up to Tom and cleared his throat, but he did not speak, and eventually he, too, walked away, leaving Tom and Tex alone.

XX

Tom did not open his eyes until noon and he never afterward recalled clearly what it was that had awakened him, but he knew that his body ached all over and his chest felt feverish.

"Tom . . .?"

It required an effort to lift his lids. When he saw her, there was movement in the background. He ignored it to concentrate full attention upon her face. "Toni."

"Are you all right, Tom?"

"I've felt somewhat better in my lifetime," he answered, propping himself up on one elbow. "I guess you heard. . . ."

"Yes."

He saw the movement again and squinted beyond her.

It was Tex and beside him stood Tim Pollard, craning his neck. Next to the sheriff was Judge Montgomery, and grouped together behind the judge were Gerald Finnerty and six or eight men he knew only by sight, local cowmen and townsmen. Prominent in their foremost rank was Roy the bartender and Grogan the liveryman. His brows drew down. "Sorry to disappoint you boys," he said dryly. "But there'll be no wake today."

Tex grinned. Roy the bartender was slower to show appreciation of Tom's poor joke. The judge remained erectly impassive; a shadow passed across his face.

Toni sat upon the edge of the bed and took his hand in hers. He winced and looked quickly at his fingers. They were purple, scabbed over, and stiff with swelling. Toni bent a long glance upon the silent men, and Sheriff Pollard was the first to understand. He edged toward the door, gouging with a sharp elbow as he passed among the others. They were nearly all out of the room when Tom said: "Judge?"

"Yes?"

"I'd like to marry your daughter."

Montgomery inclined his head. "I think that's more in her jurisdiction than in mine, Mister Barker."

"No," said Tom, holding the older man's eyes with his glance. "What I mean is, I want your approval."

The judge stood alone in the room. It seemed that words would not come, but after a moment he said: "Tom, I am not a man who is governed by swiftly changing emotions. All I can say to that is that Antoinette's judgment in this matter is better than mine, and she's satisfied you're a good man. Personally I'll have to withhold an opinion until I know you better." His gray eyes flickered. "Thus far in our acquaintanceship, Tom, quite honestly I've found you honest . . . but hard and vengeful. Those are not things I like in any man." He stopped, waiting for Tom to speak. When he did not, the judge went on. "One thing I can say, though. After due consideration those of us who have stock in the bank have decided to ask you to take Elihu Gorman's place as manager. If you haven't convinced us of much else since your return to Beatty, you've shown us you have a good business head." The judge's tone turned dry. "In that matter of hay and loans, I, at least, am well convinced of that. Will you accept? Of course, that means you'll have to stay on here. . . ."

"I accept," Tom replied.

The judge went out and softly closed the door. Toni bent fully forward and found his lips with her mouth. When she straightened up, he smiled; it was a boyish, full, and frank smile. "I'm home," he told her. "I'm back for good, Toni. Will he marry us?" She nodded through a rush of hot, unshed tears, and he lay back sighing. "Finnerty wants a neighbor. I'll take up the option next to him and give it to Tex."

"Tom?"

"Yes?"

"I suppose every woman feels this way at least once in her lifetime. . . . Tom, I love you so terribly much."

ABOUT THE AUTHOR

Lauran Paine who, under his own name and various pseudonyms has written over a thousand books, was born in Duluth, Minnesota. His family moved to California when he was at a young age and his apprenticeship as a Western writer came about through the years he spent in the livestock trade, rodeos, and even motion pictures where he served as an extra because of his expert horsemanship in several films starring movie cowboy Johnny Mack Brown. In the late 1930s, Paine trapped wild horses in northern Arizona and even, for a time, worked as a professional farrier. Paine came to know the Old West through the eyes of many who had been born in the previous century, and he learned that Western life had been very different from the way it was portrayed on the screen. "I knew men who had killed other men," he later recalled. "But they were the exceptions. Prior to and during the Depression, people were just too busy eking out an existence to indulge in Saturday-night brawls." He served in the U.S. Navy in the Second World War and began writing for Western pulp magazines following his discharge. It is interesting to note that all of his earliest novels (written under his own name and the pseudonym Mark Carrel) were published in the British market and he soon had as strong a following in that country as in the United States. Paine's Western fiction is characterized by strong plots, authenticity, an apparently effortless ability to construct situation and character, and a preference for building his stories upon a solid foundation of historical fact. *Adobe Empire* (1956), one of his best novels, is a fictionalized account of the last twenty years in the life of trader William Bent and, in an off-trail way, has a melancholy, bittersweet texture that is not easily forgotten. In later novels like *Cache Cañon* and *Halfmoon Ranch*, he showed that the special magic and power of his stories and characters had only matured along with his basic themes of changing times, changing attitudes, learning from experience, respecting Nature, and the yearning for a simpler, more moderate way of life.

The employees of Thorndike Press hope you have enjoyed this Large Print book. All our Thorndike, Wheeler, and Kennebec Large Print titles are designed for easy reading, and all our books are made to last. Other Thorndike Press Large Print books are available at your library, through selected bookstores, or directly from us.

For information about titles, please call:
(800) 223-1244

or visit our Web site at:
http://gale.cengage.com/thorndike

To share your comments, please write:
Publisher
Thorndike Press
10 Water St., Suite 310
Waterville, ME 04901